make fri̶e̶n̶d̶s̶
BRE̶AK friends

To Daisy who helped a lot.

Daisy

'What's wrong, Phoebe?' I asked. But I knew what it was.

This was about Erika and what happened after school today.

Please don't cry. Phoebe looked like a hurt puppy, hair flopping over her sad brown eyes.

'Well, let's do something,' I said briskly. 'It'll be ages before tea's ready.'

Mum was crashing around in the kitchen, still doing the breakfast pots most likely.

'What do you want to do?'

'I don't mind.'

Phoebe *never* minds. It's irritating.

'Let's do our collage then.'

Our under-the-sea scene was coming along really well and Phoebe smiled.

'That's what you wanted to do all along, isn't it?'

4

She nodded.

'So why didn't you *say*?'

Laughing, she delved into her bag and brought out some great bits of shiny material and some gauzy see-through stuff, and soon we were cutting and sticking away. I found some bits of burst balloon.

'Octopus!' we yelled at the same time.

Sometimes it's like that with Phoebe and me. We're completely on the same wavelength and don't even need to talk. We're definitely best friends. Well, I'm her only friend, actually, and that's the trouble. I'm friends with everyone, but she HATES me playing or even talking to anyone else. It drives me crazy.

'Phoebe, I was talking to Erika after school because she was upset.'

Erika had missed an open goal and the netball team had lost.

'It's my job to help people. You know that.'

I'm a school 'buddy', which means I have to help kids who are upset.

'It's your job to help people who are being *bullied*, Daisy. Erika wasn't being bullied.'

True. No one would bully Erika. She's popular and ever so funny. It's the faces she pulls. Even teachers can't help laughing. Everyone likes Erika.

Except Phoebe.

'Erika wasn't keen on going home,' I said. 'You know what her mum's like at matches.'

She SHOUTS. Today's match was in the dinner hour so she hadn't come, but Erika was dreading telling her the result.

Phoebe carried on sticking.

'So that's why I stayed talking to *her* instead of walking straight home with you.'

Phoebe and I live just round the corner from one another, but before Mum and Dad split up I lived nearer Erika. We were best friends then. Still are, in a way, but it's not the same.

6

She used to come round mine a lot.

'It doesn't mean I don't like *you* if I talk to *her*. You're both my best friends.'

Phoebe kept quiet.

'Please.' I persisted. 'Don't go all droopy when I talk to Erika. You should try and see her good points.'

'Suppose so, but what about *her*? She gets stroppy if you talk to me.'

Actually, Phoebe had a point. Erika was just as bad. Worse in a way. Phoebe wilts like a flower out of water when I play with Erika. But if Erika sees me with Phoebe she explodes. *'What do you see in her?'* Sometimes those two make me feel like a ragdoll being torn apart by two little girls in the nursery.

Idea!

It came to me in a flash. *Why don't I stop them?* I mean, if I can get little kids who've been fighting to shake hands and make up, surely I can get my two best friends to like each other?

Suddenly I was determined. It was exactly what a buddy was for – to get everyone to be friendly. Phoebe was wrong. It wasn't just about stopping bullying. Right, I was on a mission now so I needed a plan . . .

One – talk to Phoebe about Erika. Well, I'd done that.

Two – talk to Erika about Phoebe. I'll do that as soon as I can.

Three – get them to talk to each other.

It couldn't be that hard, could it?

Phoebe

I really *really* don't want to fall out with Daisy, but see *Erika's good points?*

One – she's good at games – so?

Two – she's funny – if making fun of other people is funny.

She thinks she's hilarious if she's imitating the way someone walks or talks, but it's not *kind*. And she's got a temper. She explodes if someone just spells her name wrong. *'I'm Erika with a K!'*

Three – blank.

But I'll try and think of something because I love going round Daisy's house. It's great with just her and her mum. So quiet. Not like at mine with The Smellies bawling their heads off or charging around like little tanks.

They've just learned to crawl so it's worse now as they get into my things. Why did my mum have to go and have twins?

Daisy is the best friend I've ever had. She's kind and we enjoy the same things, like art and craft, and reading and Drama Club on Friday nights. I just hope Daisy doesn't want Erika to join in with what we do. Erika doesn't *join in*. She TAKES OVER. If Daisy tells Erika about Drama Club . . . well, I don't know what I'll do, but it'll ruin everything. I hate annoying Daisy by being 'droopy', as she calls it but I can't help it. When she goes off with Erika it *hurts*, I mean *really*. It's as if my insides get tied in tight little knots.

But I'll try – well, not to let it show – or Daisy might go off me. As long as she doesn't tell me and Erika to make up, like infants in the playground.

'Shake hands and make friends, girls.'

Daisy can be very – what's the word? – bossy.

And how can you have two best friends?

Tuesday

Erika

Daisy wants me to talk to Pheeble! She cornered me in the playground straight after dinners.

I said, 'What about, Dais? We've got nothing in common.'

'You've both got two little brothers.'

I mean, what's that got to do with anything? Mum says it's having brothers that's taught me to hold my own. But Pheeble can't hold anything, definitely not a ball. She's hopeless.

'I just want you two to get to know each other,' Daisy persisted.

'But *why*?' I'd told the boys I'd play football with them.

'Because . . .'

I put my arm round her shoulders. 'Because you're a busybody-buddy who wants everyone to be luvvy-duvvy friends!'

Honestly, Daisy is so, well, *fluffy*, when she isn't being teacherish. I wish she still lived near me. It was great going round hers.

I said, 'OK, Dais, I'll promise to try and be nice to Pheeble.'

'*Don't* call her that!'

Oh, no! Now I'd upset her!

'She isn't feeble, Erika. You should get to know her and you'd see. Please, come and talk to her.'

Pheeble – whoops, Phoebe – was standing all alone by the fence.

'Not now, Dais, I promised the boys I'd play footie.'

'This afternoon then?' she persisted. 'Right?'

'Right.' I pulled my Daffy Duck face to cheer her up. 'Honest. I'll see you by the tree at playtime.'

Off at last. I must have crossed the playground in ten seconds flat.

I'll do my best but honestly I just can't see me and Phee— Whoops! – Phoebe having anything to say to each other.

Daisy

Well, I've made a start!

The meeting this afternoon went really well, thanks mostly to Erika, I have to say, though she was a bit late. I could feel Phoebe not wanting to be there, and thought she might even leave, but then Erika breezed in as friendly as anything. I was really proud of her.

'Hi, you guys! What's on the agenda?'

I had to laugh. 'It's not a council meeting, Erika!' We're both on the school council. 'But if you want to call it something I suppose it's friendship.'

I managed to explain that I like both of them and really like doing things with both of them, but it upsets me when they get jealous.

'Jealous?!' Erika wrinkled her nose. 'I'm not jealous of h—'

Phoebe went red.

'Well,' I said quickly, 'it doesn't matter what you call it. I just think it would help if you two got to know each other better.'

'OK.' Erika nodded. 'How?' She sounded really positive.

'Well, we could do things together.'

Phoebe nudged me then, but when I said, 'What is it, Phoebe?' she just looked at the ground.

Erika said, 'OK. What do you two like that I might like?'

LITTER

Pause – because I suddenly realised why Phoebe nudged me. Did I really want Erika joining in with collage or jewellery-making or our reading club? Now *I* felt myself going red.

Fortunately Phoebe helped by saying, 'What do you like doing, Erika, besides sport I mean?'

And Erika said, 'Oh, lots of things.'

But then silence again.

It was all beginning to go negative, but luckily I had a brainwave. 'Tell you what, why don't we do things together in the playground? You've seen the new grids that they painted? Well, there are all these new games we can play.'

Actually they're mostly old games, like our grannies played when they were young, but they're good fun. All the buddies have learned the rules so we can teach everyone else.

Well, we ended up playing hopscotch and Erika was best, of course, but Phoebe tried and we had some laughs.

So, fingers crossed.

Phoebe

I don't like saying this but sometimes Daisy just doesn't get it. She thinks everyone is as nice as they *seem*, and Erika isn't. Daisy thought the 'meeting' yesterday went really well. When Erika raced off she said, 'See, she was really nice!'

Well, yes, she was sort of. But by afternoon break today she was back to her old self.

Erika led her fan club into the playground. Daisy and I followed, and suddenly Erika's shouting, 'Let's play tag!' and doing 'Out scout, you're out' very fast.

Next thing I'm 'It' – surprise surprise – and she's yelling, 'Count to ten, Phoebe!' and everyone else is running away.

So there I am standing in the middle of the playground feeling, well, got at. I just knew Erika had made me 'It' on purpose, and I think

Daisy thought so too because she suddenly ran towards me.

'Tag me,' Daisy whispered. And I was going to, but then someone – no guesses who – grabs her arm and pulls her away.

'Run, Phoebe! You're supposed to run after people!' No guesses who that was, either.

But I couldn't. I just couldn't.

I know that does sound feeble but I was ever so tired. The Smellies had been bawling their heads off half the night, and I knew there was no point. I'm hopeless at running at the best of times – and, well, I didn't mean to, but I started crying in front of *everyone*, and I could feel them all staring at me.

Then Erika shouted, 'Don't be feeble, Pheeble!'

And everyone started laughing.

They *screeched* with laugher.

Everyone. Even Daisy. I saw her.

The laughing went on for ages and ages till Mrs Davies came out and sent them all inside.

Daisy

I can't believe what's just happened.

I can't believe Erika shouted what she did.

I can't believe Phoebe didn't try *at all*. She *was* feeble. I tried to help her by getting near her but she just stood there with her arms stuck out like, like a daft *windmill*.

Erika was horrible, I have to admit, but ever so funny – she pulled a face just like Phoebe's and stuck out her arms just like her – and, well, I couldn't help laughing. I *wasn't* laughing at Phoebe, I was laughing at Erika, but Mrs Davies thinks I was.

'I'm surprised at *you*, Daisy.' That's what she said before she yelled at everyone to go and stand outside her room. Then she went over to Phoebe.

Well, I just wanted to melt away. I felt sick.

Honestly, I'd have done anything to rewind the last few minutes and do it differently. But all I could do was walk up to Phoebe and say sorry. She just sobbed, 'Go away, Daisy. I thought you were my friend.'

For once Phoebe *did* mind.

And so did Mrs Davies. She shook her head and said, 'We'll talk about this later, Daisy. Go and stand with the others for the time being.'

I know she thinks I'm as bad as the others.

I'm sure she'll say I can't be a buddy any more.

Buddies are supposed to be kind!

Erika

Eeek!

I'm not sure what happened there, but I really, really didn't mean it to go like that. I chose Phoebe as 'It' to get her to join in. Honest. I was only trying to do what Daisy asked.

I just hope I managed to convince Mrs Davies, but it didn't help that Daisy looked as if she'd trodden on a kitten. I explained that it had been Daisy's idea to get Phoebe to join in more, and that I was trying to help.

Mrs D said, 'But what about the name-calling?'

'That just slipped out, Mrs Davies. A joke.'

'A cruel joke, Erika.'

I said, 'Sorry, Mrs Davies. I'll say sorry to Phoebe too.'

'Good. I'm sure you meant well, Erika.'

Exactly.

Actually I think Mrs D knows Phoebe needs to toughen up a bit. Just wish I could convince Daisy-Down-in-the-Dumps.

I tried to cheer her up when we got back to class.

'We've all apologised, Dais.' I'd organised that straight after register. 'What more can we do?'

But she exploded: 'Get lost, Miss Popular!' and stropped off to help Pheeble with her science project. Next thing she's shouting at Pheeble.

And I saw why. Honestly, there's no helping some people.

Pheeble got five merit points for work *Daisy* had done and she wouldn't tell the teacher Daisy had helped her.

Daisy was really upset so I sent her a note, saying *Still rather be friends with HER?*. And she *tore it up*.

28

Honestly, I felt myself going red. Everyone was looking at me and one of the other girls said, 'You're not going to let her get away with that, are you?'

And I said, 'No, I'm not.'

I'm really not!

Phoebe

I still feel awful.

Things are even worse now.

Daisy says she wasn't laughing at me in the playground, but I saw her. And why did she say sorry if she didn't do anything?

I thought she wanted to make up because in the next lesson she was really nice – at first. When she'd finished her science folder she came to help me with mine. I didn't actually *need* help because I'd nearly finished, but I let her help so as not to hurt her feelings.

But then she hurt mine.

When Miss Perkins gave me five merit points and said she'd show my folder to Mrs Davies, Daisy was horrible.

'Tell her! Tell her I helped you!' She *screamed*.

Well, Miss Perkins had left the room so I couldn't go running after her. I don't even know why Daisy wanted me to. I suppose she's desperate to get in Mrs Davies's good books now that she's been told off for being mean. AND, another thing, I think Daisy is jealous. I didn't think she was like that.

Afterwards I saw Erika passing her a note, so it looks as if those two are best friends again now.

Erika *is* taking over, like I knew she would.

Daisy

This afternoon was terrible.

It was horrible being told off by Mrs Davies with all the other girls. Erika may have convinced Mrs Davies she 'meant well' by choosing Phoebe to be 'It', but I'm not so sure. She definitely wasn't when she called her Pheeble.

Anyway, after break, I just got on with my work, which was finishing off our science folders. At least you can get on with your work when no one's friends with you. Well, I took my folder to Miss Perkins who said it was the *best bit of science I'd ever done*. She said it was so good she'd show my folder to Mrs Davies and I'd probably get an achievement certificate for it. Me! An achievement certificate! Erika's always getting them for sporty stuff. Phoebe gets them for all her school work, but I've never *ever* had a single one.

Well, I was cheering up a bit and went to help Phoebe with her project. But things went wrong *again*. At the end of the lesson Miss Perkins gave Phoebe five merit points, picked up *her* folder to take to Mrs Davies and left mine on the desk. I said, 'Phoebe, go and tell Miss Perkins I helped you.' But she didn't. She wouldn't. She just stood there like a frightened rabbit.

I'm SO fed up with Phoebe doing nothing. It was the playground all over again, and Erika was watching. I could almost hear her saying *'Told you so, told you so'*. Next thing she's passing me a note: *Still rather be friends with HER?*.

Well, I was furious – with both of them – so I tore it up and she went off in a massive strop.

After dinners I sensed something was wrong as soon as I stepped into the playground. I looked around to see who was in trouble –

33

and there was Erika and her fan club staring at *me*.

I was in trouble, I could feel it. You know the expression 'looking daggers'? Well, I could feel the daggers sticking into me.

Then Erika said, 'We don't like Daisy today, do we?' And they all turned their backs on me.

All of them. I can't describe the feeling exactly but it was even worse than the dagger-looks. I wanted to get away but I couldn't move.

So I just stood there feeling dreadful – like Phoebe, I suppose – when one of the dinner ladies came up and said, 'Hello, Daisy, looking for your little friend? She's in the sick room. You can go and see her if you like.'

Did I want to see Phoebe? I did actually. I'd started to feel a bit bad for having a go at her. I mean, it wasn't her fault that Miss Perkins left my folder behind. *I* could have reminded her. So I headed for the sickroom to

say, 'Sorry, Phoebe', and, 'It doesn't matter', and, 'Let's be friends'. But when I got there it was too late. She'd gone. The secretary said her mum had picked her up.

'We don't like Daisy' went on all afternoon. None of the girls spoke to me, but Miss Perkins didn't seem to notice they were being mean. Luckily, at playtime I was on buddy duty in the infants' playground. I kept busy organising a game of French cricket for some of the boys, but I couldn't stop worrying.

'I'm surprised at *you*, Daisy.' Mrs Davies's words keep going over and over in my head.

I'm really worried she's going to stop me being a buddy.

Erika

I can't stop thinking about Daisy.

Maybe I was a bit mean at school today.

I'm sure she was crying when we all turned our backs on her.

Thing is, Daisy can't bear not being friends, and actually I don't like it, either. Maybe I did overreact, but it hurt when she tore up my note. In front of everyone! When I was trying to be friendly! I thought I might blub for a minute. Anyway, tomorrow I'll tell her I forgive her and call off 'Don't speak to Daisy', and tell her I'd like to do something with her and Phoebe – just like she said she wanted to.

That should sort it. I can see her face now, all pleased and grateful.

In fact there *is* something I'd like to do with her and Phoebe. Someone said they go to a drama club on Friday nights. It's in a spooky old mill which has been converted into a theatre. Sounds really cool.

I'm going to write her a note NOW.

Thursday

Daisy

I can't *believe* Erika.

She's just given me a note saying *she's* forgiven *me* for tearing up her note! Well, you can guess what I did with that, so 'Don't talk to Daisy' is on again.

But I don't care. Well, not too much. If she thinks I'll ever be friends with her again, she's wrong, wrong, *wrong*. I'll never forgive her. Never! Phoebe's right. Erika *is* mean.

Trouble is I can't tell Phoebe because she's not here. She must still be sick. When I went round last night her mum said she'd gone to bed early. Or she's avoiding me. Phoebe's tummy aches are very convenient sometimes. Anyway, she wasn't waiting outside this morning and when I knocked on the door no one answered. Most likely no one heard. It sounded like a zoo inside. Her dad's car had gone, so at first I thought she'd had a lift to school but she wasn't in the playground when I got here.

I hope she isn't very ill.

Morning break wasn't as bad as it could have been. I went and sat on the buddy bench and Barney, who's in top class, joined me.

Barney goes to Drama Club too. It's at the Old Mill Theatre outside the village. It's not a school club. Barney was Joseph in *Joseph and his Amazing Technicolor Dreamcoat*. He's really nice and he told me something very interesting.

'Lenny says we're going to do another production, but don't tell anyone because he hasn't announced it yet.'

Lenny runs the club and Barney overheard him talking about it.

'What's the show going to be?'

'*The Wizard of Oz.*'

'Wow! Phoebe and I are reading that!'

'Cool,' he said. 'You'll know the characters really well and be great at auditions. Where is Phoebe, by the way?'

I didn't answer because I suddenly had a horrible thought. If Phoebe really has fallen

out with me I won't be able to get to Drama Club. If her mum won't take me in the car I won't be able to go.

I said, 'Can I tell Phoebe? She won't tell anyone.'

Barney laughed. 'She'd be perfect as Cowardly Lion, wouldn't she? And you'd make a great—'

But he didn't finish because Erika was rushing over.

'Hi, Daisy!' She slung her arm round me as if we were best friends. 'Hi, Barney! Tell us about this Drama Club. Can anyone join?'

Two-faced isn't the word!

I just hope Phoebe doesn't think I told her about it.

Friday

Phoebe

Daisy and I are friends again!

She came round last night and we made up. And we're going to Drama Club tonight – well, if Mum will take us. Trouble is Mum says I shouldn't go out tonight as I've been off school for two days with a bug. But I'm all right now and I've *got* to go or Daisy can't get there.

Daisy was bursting to tell me there's going to be a show. Actually, I'm not all that keen. The thing I like about Drama Club – it was such a relief when we first went – is that we *don't* have to perform. We don't even have to go on stage. We just get in pairs or groups and do improvisations, which means imagining ourselves in different situations.

I'm good at it, but if I had to do it on stage I'd die. I really would.

Still, I suppose I can say I'd rather work backstage. Yes, that's what I'll do. I'll volunteer to make props or help with the costumes. I could even design some. I'd like that.

I'm really enjoying *The Wizard of Oz*, reading the book I mean, and I've nearly finished it. Daisy thinks it's a bit slow, but I think it will make a great show, and she'd be ace as Dorothy. I'd just love her to get the main part so I'm going to try my hardest to persuade Mum to take us. In fact I'll remind Mum she owes Daisy. Mum had nagged me to join the Drama Club for ages – to '*bring me out*', she said – but I didn't dare till Daisy said she'd go with me.

I'm so glad we're friends again.

Daisy

Trouble! Erika came to Drama Club last night!

I hadn't dared tell Phoebe that Erika had asked Barney about joining. I just hoped Erika would forget all about it, but when we got to the Old Mill she was there with a crowd around her, laughing at one of her jokes.

It was just like school.

'Hi, Daisy! Hi, Phoebe!' She waved when she saw us.

Well, Phoebe just froze in the doorway. I nearly had to drag her inside.

Still, I don't think Erika liked it much. I'm sure she was expecting to be a star, instantly. When Lenny asked us to get in twos and think of something we were scared of she started sucking her thumb and stuttering, 'I'm s-s-scared of the b-b-bogeyman.'

Everyone laughed till Lenny told us to go away and find a space and have a quiet think. Later, I saw Lenny having a word with her and guessed what he was saying. *'Stop playing to the gallery, Erika.'* That's what he says to anyone who's showing off and looking for applause.

Phoebe saw too but it didn't stop her wailing, *'Why* did you tell her?'

I said, 'I didn't – and, look, she probably won't come again now she's seen what it's like.'

If Lenny had told me off the first time I went I'd never have shown my face again.

But Erika's not like me – or anyone else I know. I suppose she's used to being criticised by her mother. Anyway, she was soon bouncing around again like Tigger!

Actually, and I couldn't say this to Phoebe, but a bit of me can't help admiring that.

Erika

Drama Club's great!

Well, it will be when we start rehearsing for a proper show. At first it was a bit boring because we did 'exploring your emotions' and everyone was dead serious, but then, halfway through, Lenny the director said we were going to do *The Wizard of Oz*, actually put it on for an audience! Well, I just LOVE that show and when I told Mum on the way home she said, 'You'd make a great Dorothy, darling.'

'But that's the main part, Mum, and I've only just started.'

'Aim high, darling. You don't want to be an also-ran, do you?'

Well, she's right, actually. I think I'm in with a chance because we've got the DVD and I've seen it hundreds of times. Also, well, I don't want to be big-headed, but none of the others seemed very good at acting. Except Barney, but he can't very well be Dorothy, can he?

Everyone was friendly except Daisy and Pheeb— Whoops! – Phoebe. They didn't seem at all pleased to see me, which was a bit off. I mean it was Daisy's idea that we started doing things together. Those two hold grudges. That's their trouble. Forgive and forget, that's what I say.

Anyway, the auditions are next week so I'm going to start practising.

Saturday

Phoebe

I'm up and down like a seesaw.

UP. I *do* want a part. I'll show Erika. She's *not* going to ruin Drama Club.

DOWN. I don't want to go any more.

Last night was just like school. Honestly, when I walked in and saw her there, the centre of attention already, I wanted to be sick. If it wasn't for Daisy I'd have stayed outside, but she said, 'Come *on* – unless you're determined to let her take over.'

But all night long I could feel her thinking I was rubbish.

But – UP – I *am* good at acting. I *can* imagine what it's like being someone else and that's what acting is, unless – DOWN – other people are watching.

But – UP– at least I'm not afraid of my own mother like someone I could mention.

Anyway, Lenny says we've all got to audition for a part, even if we do just want to work behind the scenes, so I'm going to have to try. And I'm going to help Daisy practise so she gets a good part. I'm going round hers this morning to discuss the characters. Daisy and I are going to act some bits out too.

Six days to find my courage!

Friday

A Week Later

Daisy

Auditions tonight!

I'm nervous but also quite optimistic because the rest of today was great. My confidence is well boosted. It started just after register when Miss Perkins said I'd got an achievement certificate for my science project! Really! She remembered, after all, with a bit of help from Phoebe she said. But Phoebe hadn't told me she'd reminded her.

'Phoebe, why didn't you tell me you'd told her?'

'So you'd get a surprise,' she said with this big smile on her face – till Erika came along to say congratulations.

I was scared of going to Mrs Davies's room to get it, but Phoebe came with me to get hers too, and Mrs Davies was really nice. I still thought she might say I couldn't be a buddy any more because I'd laughed at Phoebe, but she didn't.

She just said, 'It's good to see that you two are friends again.'

I said, 'We didn't stop being friends, Mrs Davies.'

I just wish I could say the same about Erika and Phoebe. My mission to get us all to be friends has failed miserably. It's the same old problem – I can be friends with one or the other. I mean Phoebe and I are getting on really well at the moment, and Erika's been nice all week. There's been no more 'Don't talk to Daisy'. Quite the opposite, in fact. Everyone's been friendly but if I speak two words to Erika, Phoebe still droops.

No, actually she doesn't now. She *hisses*.

It's a mini-explosion and quite funny.

Except that I feel bad about Erika who wants, no *needs*, a lift home with us after Drama Club. I told her I'd talk to Phoebe about it, but I haven't – yet.

Erika

Time's running out.

Thing is, I can't go to Drama Club tonight unless I can get a lift home, well to my gran's, because Mum and Dad are going to the rugby club dance. They're taking my brothers to Gran's earlier.

I suppose I need to talk to Phoebe myself – though Daisy said she would – but Phoebe's not speaking. Not to me, anyway. I've tried to be nice to her all week. I asked both of them round to my house to see my *The Wizard of Oz* DVD, and I think Daisy was going to say yes till Phoebe sort of snorted and said she has it.

I asked Daisy on Wednesday if I could have a lift home with her because my mum can only take me, but she said her mum hasn't got a car now. She always gets a lift with Phoebe both ways *and* she was having a sleepover with Phoebe this Friday.

Daisy said she'd get back to me. But here it is, Friday afternoon, and she still hasn't.

At break I asked Barney if I could have a lift with him but he said his dad's car is full already. I said I was nervous about the audition. He laughed – as if he didn't believe me – and said there'll be parts for everyone and no one will be left out. Trouble is – I couldn't say this – I don't want *any* part. Actually, I think Mum's gone off Drama Club now she's realised there will be loads of extra rehearsals to go to – on top of all my matches and practices – and she definitely won't want to take me if I'm only a Munchkin or a Winkie or a Winged Monkey.

Barney said I'd make a good Wicked Witch of the West.

I'm beginning to think he doesn't like me.

Daisy

I've been a chicken.

After school I managed to leave without talking to Erika.

But I soon wished I hadn't snuck out because right at the last minute Phoebe's dad sent a text to her mum saying he was stuck at work with the car. So she couldn't take us to Drama Club.

'Can't take us?' Phoebe *wailed*. 'But, Mum, you've got to!'

Well, I'd have wailed too if I'd been at home but, as I wasn't, I racked my brain for a solution and said, 'We'll have to ask Erika. She did offer.'

Well, Phoebe shook her head as if I'd suggested going in a car with a boa constrictor, but I told her, 'It's Erika or nothing.'

And, hoping it wasn't too late, we got

Phoebe's mum to ring Erika's – while we tried to keep The Smellies quiet by building brick towers for them to knock down. Actually, they were quite sweet.

Soon there was a knock on the door and Erika was on the doorstep looking ever so pleased. Her mum was outside in their car and Phoebe and I piled in the back. Erika was chatty and I did my best to chat back, even though I could feel Phoebe glowering at me.

The auditions were fun – nerve-racking but fun. At first we did some loosening-up exercises, then Lenny asked us to try different characters. He asked Phoebe to read the part of Cowardly Lion who wanted more than anything to be brave and Erika to try the part of the Tin Woodman who needs a heart. The thought *typecasting* came into my head when he asked me to try for Scarecrow.

All three of us did well, that's what I thought, and I think Lenny did too because he called us back to read a bit more. We had to do part of a scene together and by the end of it we were working well as a team – even Phoebe. Well, she was so into the part of Cowardly Lion, I think she forgot it was Erika being Tin Woodman.

It wasn't until later that things started to go wrong. The session had ended and we were outside waiting for Phoebe's dad to pick us up. I suddenly realised we were the last ones waiting and that it was ever so dark. Clouds covered the moon and the stars. The only light was a dim yellow lamp flickering above the door, and the wind was howling through the bare branches of some nearby trees. From time to time, when the wind dropped, you could hear water hitting the sides of the mill with an eerie splash, but you couldn't see the pond. You couldn't see where it began. All you could see, every now and again, was a jerky shadow on the mill wall. *A tree,* I told myself, though sometimes it looked like a person.

Looking out for Phoebe's dad's car I saw a pair of red tail-lights moving down the track towards the road. Then they disappeared and there were no more after that, and no headlights coming in the opposite direction.

We were alone by a mill which some people said was haunted. Rubbish, of course, but . . .

Phoebe

We waited for ages.

I felt awful. I mean it was my dad we were waiting for. What had happened? Surely he must have left work by now?

Daisy was unusually quiet. So was Erika. In the end I said, 'I can't think where Dad's got to. Sorry.'

Erika sounded cross. 'It's freezing out here. We'd better go inside and tell Lenny.'

But Lenny had gone already. I knew he had, and when Erika tried the door – she didn't believe me, of course – she found it was locked, and Daisy said she remembered seeing him outside earlier.

'He must have thought we'd been picked up when we went to the outside loo.'

As far as we could see, which wasn't very far, there were no cars left in the car park.

My tummy started squirgling as if something bad was going to happen.

'OK.' Erika waved her mobile as if it was the answer to everything. 'There's obviously been a mix-up over times. We need to ring home – *your* home, Phoebe. What's your number?'

But when she tried to ring she couldn't get a signal and I remembered other people had said their phones didn't work here. Neither Daisy nor I had mobiles, and I started to feel panicky.

Daisy was making a big effort to keep calm, I could tell. And Erika was still being team captain.

'Right, we need a plan.' Erika looked at her watch. 'It's nine o'clock. There's obviously been a hitch. Who usually meets you guys?'

I said it was usually Mum, but Dad was going to come straight from work this evening.

'Right. That's it, isn't it?' Erika sounded super-confident. 'I bet your dad doesn't know he has to come right down the track to the mill to get us. So he's parked on the road, waiting for us. We'll just have to walk up there.'

I had to agree, though I hated being bossed around by *her*.

I said, 'We'll have to be careful we don't fall in the pond.'

There were railings round it but some of them were broken – and there was something else.

Peg Powler.

It's just a stupid legend about this girl who drowned in olden times . . . but the shadow on the mill wall kept making me think she might be around. She has these long arms and—

Enough of that! I just knew I wanted to get as far away as possible, so I set off after Erika.

Erika

'Come on, Phoebe.' I *didn't* call her Pheeble even though she looked like a frightened rabbit. 'Let's go and look for your dad.'

Anything was better than standing there doing nothing, thinking about . . . *Peg Powler* . . .

They both agreed that walking to the road was the best option, though neither of them said *Thank you, Erika. What a good idea.*

It was about half a mile, I reckoned, and would take about ten minutes. Well, it would take *me* about ten minutes. I set off at a brisk pace, hoping the other two would be able to keep up, when I tripped and hurt my foot.

Hurt isn't the word. I couldn't believe the pain. The *agony*. Or the embarrassment. I felt so stupid.

One second I was striding forward, leading

the other two. Next I was writhing on the ground with the pair of them looking down at me.

To my amazement Phoebe took charge. 'Don't move. You mustn't put any weight on the foot. It might be broken.' She'd done first aid in Brownies, she said. 'We must get help.'

Daisy was worried. 'We can't just leave her here, can we?'

'No, don't leave me!' I hated myself for crying out, but my head hurt too and, well, I didn't want to scare the others, but it was really spooky. I was sure I could see something moving by the pond.

'Erika, we're *not* going to leave you.' Daisy sounded cross, but Phoebe was more sympathetic. She was kneeling by my foot.

'Ow!' She touched it.

'Sorry, but it may just be sprained, not broken. If it is, maybe you could walk to the road if we took your weight?'

But when I got to my feet with their help it was still agony. There was no way I could walk that far.

'W-we'll have to go back to the mill then,' said Daisy.

She didn't sound too keen.

Nor did Phoebe. 'And h-hope for the best and that my dad comes soon. I expect he'll come looking when we don't turn up.'

I knew I should say *Just leave me here and go for help*, but I couldn't. I was sure the eerie splashing from the pond was getting louder.

The mill was about fifty metres away and we could see the yellow light glimmering. I managed to hop on my good foot with my arms round their shoulders – they nearly carried me – and when we got to the door, they lowered me carefully to the ground. Daisy got her pyjamas out of her backpack and made a cushion for my hurt foot.

Daisy said, 'Let's all look in our bags and see what else we've got.'

Soon we had a pile consisting of pyjamas; a gym shirt; gym shorts; several books, including *The Wizard of Oz*; and a squashed Mars Bar, which we shared. I insisted we shared.

Phoebe made sure we put on all the extra clothes to keep warm.

'Especially you, Erika. You must keep warm in case of shock. Put Daisy's gym kit on over your clothes.'

I must have looked like a scarecrow, but I didn't care.

Just hoped I'd scare any spooks.

Daisy

Peg Powler.

Whenever it went silent – I mean if we stopped talking – I couldn't help thinking about her. You could hear the wind howling. Or maybe a ghostly voice? Peg Powler is a legend, a drowned girl, a ghost – I may as well say it – who's supposed to hide in the pond under the slime. Sometimes, people say, she reaches out with her long white arms and grabs passers-by.

To drown them. As revenge for something.

Not true. A story. I told myself. *A ghost story. I don't believe in ghosts.*

Luckily we didn't stop talking for long, because Phoebe said the two of us must keep Erika awake in case she had concussion. Phoebe really was a heroine, a proper Florence Nightingale.

Anyway, we sat either side of Erika and talked and played games and took it in turns to read bits from *The Wizard of Oz*, which helped keep our spirits up. Luckily the light over the door stayed on – as long as we waved our arms every now and again. It was the only light because the moon stayed behind thick clouds.

Erika was brave too. I could see she was in pain but she hardly ever complained. She jumped once when a loud splashing sound came from the pond – we all did – but none of us said what we were thinking. We all kept a lookout for Phoebe's dad's car and longed to see it coming towards us. Once we thought we saw car headlights go past in the distance, on the road, but it got harder and harder to see that far. It was getting foggy. That was the trouble. It was as if the clouds were descending. Soon we could see mist *rolling* towards us, billowing like smoke but cold and wet.

I was thinking that November must be the most horrible month in the year when I saw this shape rise up and come looming out of the darkness, this human shape with arms outstretched and enormous hands . . .

Had the others seen it?

'*Aaagh!*' I know I cried out.

I think we all did because next thing we were clinging together, watching whatever it was coming nearer and nearer . . .

Then Erika's voice came out of the darkness saying something rude that meant, 'Go away.' I must have closed my eyes by then, and I remember thinking she was very brave – or silly to annoy the creature.

Then Phoebe started to laugh or cry in great gulping sobs. I forced myself to open my eyes and saw these huge hands gripping her shoulders . . .

Phoebe

'D-d-dad!'

I recognised him first, of course, though, like the others, when I saw him coming towards us with arms outstretched I thought it was the ghost coming to get us!

It seemed ages before I noticed the sleeves of his coat. Tweed without a speck of green slime. I couldn't help screaming, 'Dad! Where have you *been*?'

Then, I have to admit, I burst into tears.

Poor Dad. He felt awful especially when we told him about Erika's injury. 'It's been one disaster after another,' he said. He'd got the time wrong – half an hour late. He'd got the pick-up place wrong, as Erika had guessed, and when he did decide that he ought to drive right down to the mill, the car wouldn't start.

'But don't worry, girls, one of my mates is on his way here in his car. I rang him. We'll go straight to the hospital. What's your parents' number, Erika?'

Three Weeks Later

Daisy

It was the Best and Worst Night of My Life. I don't need to tell you why it was the worst, and you may have guessed why it was the best.

Because it changed things.

Well, you can't go through a night like that and not be changed. I think Erika and Phoebe learned to respect each other.

But it's more than that.

I didn't realise how different things were till a few weeks later when I got to school late because I'd been to the dentist. It was break, and everyone was in the playground. I scanned the yard to see who was around and spotted Erika and Phoebe, heads close together. When I got nearer I saw they were swapping Moshi cards and heard them giggling. Erika and Phoebe were giggling! Together!

And do you know what? I felt just the tiniest bit jealous and left out, till they saw me and called me over.

Actually, they've both been really friendly to me – and each other – since that night. We even play together sometimes and, when I do play with just one of them, I can't hear any hissy fits.

Oh, another thing – we all got good parts in the play. Phoebe got Cowardly Lion, Erika got

Tin Woodman and best bit last – I got Dorothy, AND they both seemed really pleased for me! We're having loads of fun rehearsing. So my plan to get my two best friends to be friendly worked after all.

Mission accomplished!

A Friend in Need!

For Hattie and Phoebe, great nieces!

Thursday

Daisy

Erika's not talking to me.

At school I put a note in her drawer saying, 'What's the matter? PLEASE let's talk.' But she didn't answer. And I've just texted, 'Shall I come round?' But she hasn't texted back.

Perhaps she didn't find my note? Actually, I didn't see her go to her drawer before the bell went and she had to rush off to a match or race, or something.

Maybe I'm worrying too much.

But Erika's not talking to Phoebe, either. And Phoebe isn't answering my texts. I know she thinks I'm worrying too much about Erika, but Phoebe doesn't know Erika like I do. They didn't used to get on, but I've sorted that out. We've all been friends for weeks now.

Now it looks as if they've both gone off *me*. So I'm stuck in my bedroom with no one to talk to except Marmalade, and he's fast asleep. Mum's downstairs but she'd just tell me not to worry if I told her. I suppose I could go round Phoebe's, but what if Erika comes here while I'm there?

The reason I'm worried about Erika is that I think she's in some sort of trouble. She's been acting really strangely. But why won't she tell me what it is? I wouldn't tell anyone – well not unless she's in *danger*. I wouldn't even tell Phoebe if Erika didn't want me to. Although that would upset Phoebe if she found out. But I'm really trustworthy and sensible. Everyone says so. That's why I'm a school buddy.

Oh, dear. How am I going to find out what's bugging Erika? I hate it when we're not speaking.

Phoebe

I'm fed up with Daisy going on and on about Erika. It's all she ever talks – or texts – about at the moment. And we're only supposed to use our new mobiles for emergencies.

Erika really hurt my feelings today. I took in my spare Moshi cards to do a swap and she didn't even look at them. She just looked as if she'd been turned into a horrible Glump and went off to practise shooting at goal. That's probably what it's about in fact. When Erika's got a match coming up it's bye-bye to her non-sporty friends till it's all over. She's SO sporty!

Oh no, here's another text from Daisy.

MUST FIND WHATS UP WTH E

Why? It's not a mystery. Erika's good fun except when she's got a race or a match or a tournament. Then she's just BORING. It's train train train.

I'm texting Daisy.

**PLEASE CAN WE GET
ON WTH OUR PROJECT?**

We're designing a set for our next show at Drama Club, *The Thwarting of Baron Bollingrew*. I've got this cardboard box which will make a great medieval castle IF – quick, close door! – I can get it to Daisy's before my little brothers wreck it. That's another thing, Erika's decided not to be in this show. And we really need her because there are fifteen parts and only twelve of us to act them, as well as all the men at arms and poor and needy villagers. Erika would make a great Mike Magpie. I can just see her hopping all over the stage making everyone laugh. Daisy thinks so too, so we're both going to text her and say she's GOT to be in it.

Oh no, more trouble. The Smellies are bawling their heads off. Enter Mum any moment now to blame me. Honestly, nothing's going right at the moment.

Erika

Oh, dear. I know I'm upsetting Dais and Phoebe, but what else can I do? I've got to deal with this myself. But if I see Dais and Phoebe I'll blab, I know I will. It will all come pouring out and they'll start treating me like some poor little kid who's fallen over in the playground.

I can hear Daisy now. 'You're being *bullied,* Erika!'

No, Dais, I'm NOT! It's just some stupid person trying to scare me off winning.

AND Daisy would insist we tell a teacher which would make things a trillion zillion times worse. I mean it's most likely someone just joking. They'd laugh their heads off if I made a fuss about it. Me? Bullied? I don't think so. I'm not a wimpy loser and I'm absolutely not scared by a few texts. The thing to do is keep quiet, play it cool. Then they won't even know if I'm getting the texts.

But I really wish I knew who was sending them. Trouble is the cowardy custard is hiding SENT BY. How do they do that? And how have they got my number? Oh no, here's another one.

YR NOT LIST-NIN R U?

That must be because I won all my heats tonight. I'm fastest in the county! And here's another.

OK. LET U OF THIS TIME
BUT LOOSE 3 SHYRES

Aha! A clue! The creep can't spell. AND they want to win the Three Counties' Cross Country even more than I do. But, no, that's not a clue. Everyone wants to win. I mean, why run if you don't? Well, whoever the creep is they don't know me if they think a few texts can scare me off! I'm going for a run right now.

'Come on, Rolly!'

98

But better text Daisy first. Super-sensitive Dais has sensed something's wrong so I'll just say everything's hunky dory.

NOTHING UP JUST FOCUSSED ON RACE. C U IN MORNING.

'Come on, Rolly. Wake up. We're in training!'

Friday

Daisy

Phew! Panic over. Last night I had a cheery text from Erika – saying she's in training for the cross country finals. So, Phoebe's right, that's why she's been a bit off lately. It's not because she's avoiding us. She's just focussed on her running.

Phoebe's still grumpy though. I went round hers last night and she said Erika should think of other people more, but I can see why Erika doesn't want to be in the Drama Club show. This is a really big race for her.

Anyway, I think I managed to cheer Phoebe up. We got on with the model of the set. Then we had a bit of a clothes swap. I lent Phoebe my sparkly pumps and she lent me her new skirt. And I brought the model home with me to keep it safe from the Smellies.

Oh, Marmalade's woken up. I thought I heard a dog barking. 'It's OK, Marmalade, it's only Erika and Rolly and he's nice to cats.' He's on one of those long leads anyway. They're running past our house. Well Erika is, she's miles ahead! Poor old Rolly obviously wants to stop, but she doesn't.

Erika didn't even wave. Never mind. We're still friends, that's the main thing, and when this race is over, we'll get back to normal.

Drama Club tonight – my fave night of the week! I'd better get round to Phoebe's as her mum's taking us.

Erika

'Well, Rolly, didn't today go well? Think I deserve an Oscar after today's performance. Dais and Phoebe were well taken in, and if Secret Sender was watching he or she would be well miffed to see me so upbeat. I didn't see anyone at school giving me evil looks so I'm pretty sure it isn't anyone there. No more texts today so SS must have got the message – DON'T MESS WITH ERIKA!

'This is just between you and me, Rolly. Luckily I can tell you anything, or I'd burst, but I'm sure it's best not to tell the others. Sometimes I think you're the cuddliest-wuddliest best friend I've got. Sorry, though, I've got to leave you here tomorrow morning as I'm running with Mum. She thinks I should step up the training and says you slow me down.'

Better get some sleep now. Oh, here's another text!

PLEASE PLEASE PLEASE
BE IN THE PLAY, E!!!

Phew! It's from Daisy. And here's another.

NOT SAME WITHOUT YOU!!!

That's Phoebe. They must have just got back from Drama Club.

OH, I hate disappointing them but I really really have to put *everything* I've got into winning the Three Counties. Mum says there might be *national* coaches there and if I win they may select me to run for the *country*, or at least join their training sessions. I mean, I could be heading for the next Olympics! That's better than a poxy play.

SORRY GIRLS GOT MORE
IMPORTANT THINGS TO DO!!!

Saturday

Phoebe

I can't believe what Erika texted last night. There I was really missing her and telling her so. Then we got that rude message back. Now I'm glad she's not going to be in the play. We'll manage without her. Erika's not just rude, she's insulting. But Daisy doesn't seem to mind! She says Erika's being jokey and that I haven't got a sense of humour and that's the big difference between Erika and me, and the sooner I get a sense of humour the better.

Cheek!

When she came round this afternoon I said, 'Daisy, please tell me why does Erika think what she's doing is more important than what we're doing?' And Daisy sighed dramatically and said, 'She doesn't, not really. It was a joke. J-O-K-E.'

She says Erika is always joking and the thing to do is joke back. I said I think we should ignore her but Daisy's texting Erika now.

YOULL BE SORRY IF YOU DON'T!!!

I said, 'What are you going to do to her if she doesn't?'

And she rolled her eyes and said, 'Nothing of course, I'm J-O-K-I-N-G.'

Sometimes those two make me feel really left out.

Erika

A text from Dais! What does she mean though? YOULL BE SORRY IF YOU DON'T!!!

That doesn't sound friendly.

And here's another.

GLAD U LEFT MUT BEHIND

What does she mean by that? Oh no, this one's not from Dais. It's from Secret Sender! Or – just had a thought – I mean could Daisy BE the secret sender? Could Daisy and Phoebe both be? Whoever it is saw me running with Rolly yesterday and then without Rolly today, when I went running with Mum, and I do run past Daisy's house. Yes! It must be her. It's obvious. She must have just forgotten to delete sender with that 'YOU'LL BE SORRY' one. So that's it! Mystery solved! Phew! Dais's miffed because I've dropped out of Drama Club and because I'm not doing stuff with her and Phoebe all the time. So I was right all along. It *is* a joker, but only Dais. Double phew! I'm so glad I didn't make a fuss. She'd have laughed her head off.

And here's another. Oh, now she's going too far.

LOOSE RASE OR WILL GET YR MUT

Does she really think that's funny? Well, I don't. It's horrible. No one threatens Rolly and gets away with it. Daisy had better look out!

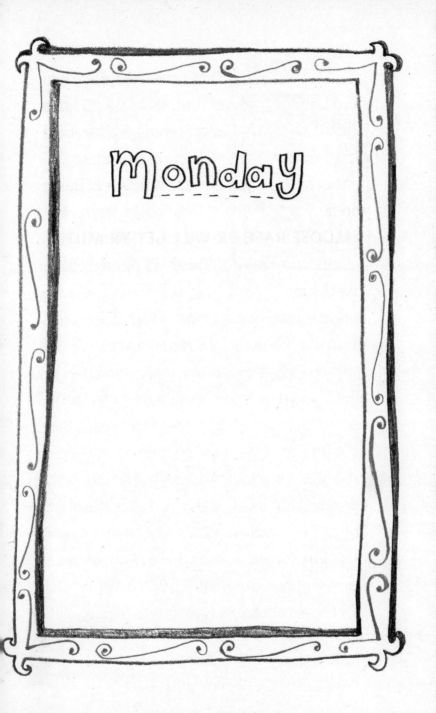

Monday

Phoebe

Daisy and Erika have had a terrible bust-up. Erika was waiting by the gate when we got to school and she just flew at Daisy.

'How could you? How could you?' She *screamed*.

Daisy said, 'It was a joke, Erika.'

'Some joke! Threatening Rolly!' Then Erika stormed off into the playground where all the sporty girls gathered round. Next thing they're all looking daggers at Daisy, who's mystified.

Daisy was in a right state. Obviously her little joke misfired, but she didn't know what Erika was on about, about threatening Rolly I mean. Nor did I. Daisy hadn't threatened Rolly. Daisy would never do anything like that. But someone must have. And because Daisy sent her jokey YOU'LL BE SORRY IF YOU DON'T text, Erika thought it was her.

Well, I decided I'd talk to Erika, after I'd tried to get Daisy to calm down. I'd never seen her so upset or so negative. She's the one who's always telling me off for being negative, but she was saying that we couldn't work it out if Erika wouldn't talk to us. Daisy was sure Erika would never ever talk to her again. She was devastated that Erika could even *think* she'd threaten Rolly.

I managed to get Daisy to stop crying before we went into school and at break she was on buddy duty in the infants' playground. So I went to find Erika by myself – hoping she wouldn't see me shaking in my shoes, well Daisy's sparkly pumps.

Honestly, though, I was nervous. Erika can be shouty.

I found her by the scooter park with some of her other friends, most of the netball team, and she said, 'I'm not talking to you, Pheeble, not if you're still friends with *her.*'

She used to call me Pheeble before we became friends.

I could see Daisy in the infants' playground and so could Erika. I think she'd been watching her. Anyway I took a deep breath and came right out with it.

'You've got it all wrong, Erika. Daisy sent you one text as a joke.' And I explained what had happened.

Erika didn't look convinced, but then her

mobile went *ping*. Another text. She read it, looked across at Daisy, and frowned.

'What does it say?' I asked. She showed it to me.

NOT JOCKING LOOSE
3C OR DOG GETS IT

I said, 'That wasn't Daisy, Daisy can spell. And look at her.' But I didn't need to. Erika could see Daisy playing hopscotch with some little kids. Her mobile was nowhere in sight.

'W-who was it then?' Her voice was a sort of trembly mumble. I think she was upset and a bit ashamed. 'Th-that's the second time they've threatened him.'

I said, 'Who has?'

'Don't know, do I?' she snapped, stroppy Erika now. 'That's the trouble. The creep deletes SENT BY. If I knew who it was I'd go right round and get them. I'd, I'd—'

Another text came in and she showed it to me.

WE NO U R READIN THIS

Someone was watching us – and texting. It was a really weird feeling. We both looked around the playground then to see who it might be – but I couldn't see anyone with a mobile, though they could be hiding it.

Daisy was staring at us now.

I wanted to beckon her over, but said, 'What does 3C mean?'

'Three Counties,' Erika wailed. 'Someone

wants me to lose the Three Counties Cross-Country finals at the end of the month. But what do they mean by "the dog gets it"?'

I could see from her face that she was picturing something horrible being done to Rolly.

I said, 'No one would hurt Rolly, Erika. I mean, you couldn't.'

Honestly, I'm not particularly doggy, but when Rolly looks at me with his big soulful eyes I can feel myself going all ah-ish.

'*You* couldn't,' she said. 'And . . . Daisy couldn't, but some people are cruel.'

I took that as my cue to call Daisy over and we had a group hug with lots of sorries, then Erika told us the whole story. It had started five days ago with a text SLO DOWN OR ELS just before the County Cross Country final.

'Since then they've got nastier.' She showed us the texts.

Daisy said, 'Erika, this is serious. We've got

to tell a grown-up.'

Erika grabbed Daisy's arm. 'NO, Dais! Don't!'

Then the bell rang and I said, 'Let's keep it to ourselves for the mo and talk about it again at dinner. Meanwhile let's all keep watch and see if we can find out who texted WE NO U R READIN THIS. It must be someone in school.

'There's no need to panic. It's two weeks to the Three Counties race. I know we'll be able to work it out before then.'

Erika

I feel better for telling Dais and Phoebe – and finding out that Secret Sender wasn't Dais. I don't know how I could have thought it really. Just shows what a state I was in. Phoebe's right – I've got to keep calm. Just hope Dais doesn't blab to a teacher.

There would probably be an assembly about it and I'd look a complete idiot. *Ha ha, Erika's being bullied.* And Mrs Davies would tell Mum who'd charge in fists flying and SS would dive for cover and we'd never find out.

Actually, this is worse than bullying, it's blackmail, and the important thing is to FIND OUT WHO'S DOING THIS. For Rolly's sake.

I'm going to watch everyone in class very carefully.

Daisy

It's maths and there's a lot of watching going on. Some of Erika's other friends are giving me hard stares. Erika's being a bit obvious staring at one person for about a minute and then moving on to the next. She isn't concentrating on the lesson at all, which is unusual for her. Her hand's usually up and down like a yoyo.

And someone else is watching her. Callum. Mind you, he never concentrates in lessons. Miss Perkins is always shouting at him to get on with his work. But he's concentrating now – on Erika. But why? He's not even a runner.

Actually several people are watching Erika, probably wondering what's wrong with her. She's acting so out of character. I think watching isn't enough. We need a real plan of action.

Tuesday

Phoebe

Daisy's turned detective! She thinks we can solve this mystery, but I think we should just tell a grown-up.

I mean by not telling we could be putting Rolly's life in DANGER.

Why doesn't Erika want to tell anyone? What's wrong with saying you're being bullied? I suppose Erika thinks she'll look like a loser, but it's better than being bullied.

Anyway, Detective Daisy had this plan for both of us to go to Athletics Club with Erika, to one of her training sessions, tonight. But I didn't think my mum would let me, and she didn't. So Daisy's gone by herself, well, with Erika, who's told her mum that Daisy wants to cheer her on. But Daisy's really going to watch all the other runners to see who's desperate to win. She thinks if she finds someone who

124

wants to win even more than Erika does it might be the secret sender. I said look at the parents too and see if any of them shout louder than Erika's mum.

Mum wouldn't let me go because she wanted me to help with the Smellies at bath time.

They're being little horrors at the mo, even worse than usual. I was brill with them so at least I'm in Mum's good books, but I can't help wondering how Daisy's getting on.

Daisy

It was boring and exhausting! *I* had to run! Erika's mum insisted. It wouldn't have been so bad if Erika was one of the sprinters. They hung around a lot between races, but cross country is all about stamina so they run for ages. I don't know how many circuits I did but I'm sure I ran a marathon. It wasn't even a race, just training, but Erika was way ahead of the others all the way and she put this spurt on at the end and everyone cheered. I could hear them, even though I was miles behind.

When I got off the track I tried to tune in to what people were saying – after I got my breath back – but I only heard praise for Erika, except from her mum. She had this huge stop watch and kept saying that Erika's time was actually rather slow and she needed someone to challenge her.

It seems Ashley, the boy who usually does, was away.

I'm beginning to think this plan won't work, either. I mean, everyone seemed really happy for Erika, except her mum, but her mum wouldn't send her threatening texts.

At least I can see why Erika likes Athletics Club. She's really popular there. There's a team of four running in the Three Counties and two of the others were there – one girl, one boy – but Erika was definitely the star.

I think we need a different tactic. I'm going to ask Phoebe. She's the one with the clever ideas.

Thursday

Erika

Phoebe thinks I should tell the POLICE! So does Daisy! Typical! I knew those two would go OTT. I should never have told them. I've forbidden them of course – to tell *anyone* – but Phoebe had this 'brilliant' idea that the police could hack into the phone, find out who's threatening me and go round and sort them out. Well, that would be great except that *everyone* would know!

Actually, it's three days since the last text so it looks like Secret Sender has given up. Oh, I really can't waste any more time on this. I've got to concentrate on winning. Mum will go ballistic if I don't improve my times. I run faster when I have someone to pace myself against so I asked Ashley to come round tonight.

When I rang him his dad answered and he sounded horrible. I heard him call out, 'Your girlfriend wants to put you through your paces, Ash. Are you up to it?'

No wonder Ashley sounded nervous, but he said he thought meeting up and running together was a great idea. He said he needed

to get back in training because he's had a bug and been off for a few days. That's why he missed Tuesday night.

Only one drawback, Rolly will have to come with us. I don't see how else I can manage to take him for a walk and fit in netball practice after school. Just hope I don't have to keep stopping to fill poo-bags. That would be SO embarrassing.

'No poos, Rolly!'

Friday

Phoebe

Callum's definitely watching Erika. He hardly lets her out of his sight. And it's not just in school. When I told Daisy I was sure he was looking at Erika in school she punched the air as if she'd just won the lottery. She'd noticed it too. We really are super sleuths!

Another thing – I checked Callum's spelling. It's awful.

The question is: *why is he watching her?* Anyway we decided to try and see if he watches her outside of school as well. First we hung around at home-time and observed he went off in the same direction as Erika usually does, though she didn't last night because of netball. Daisy said he lives quite near Erika, so he could follow her easily. She used to live at that end too.

On the way home Daisy and I discussed the

all-important *why*. I said, 'Daisy, you don't think Callum could, like, *love* Erika do you?'

Daisy said, 'Boys in our year do not love *girls*, Phoebe. They love football, computer games, and possibly designer trainers but girls NO.'

But later on Daisy texted me:

LOOK OUT OF WINDOW!!!

Daisy

I could hardly believe it – not just Erika and Rolly running by with a boy I didn't know, but also Callum, *lurking.* Following them. I'm sure of it, because though he was looking in the window of the paper-shop, pretending to read the notices, once they'd passed he set off after them lickety-split. Phoebe texted seconds later to say she'd seen first them, then him, go past her house.

Of course Phoebe thinks this proves Callum's in love with Erika, but I still don't. There must be some other reason.

Today we told Erika what we'd noticed and of course asked her who she was running with. She said it was the boy from the Athletics Club who was missing on Tuesday night. His name's Ashley and he's her closest rival and

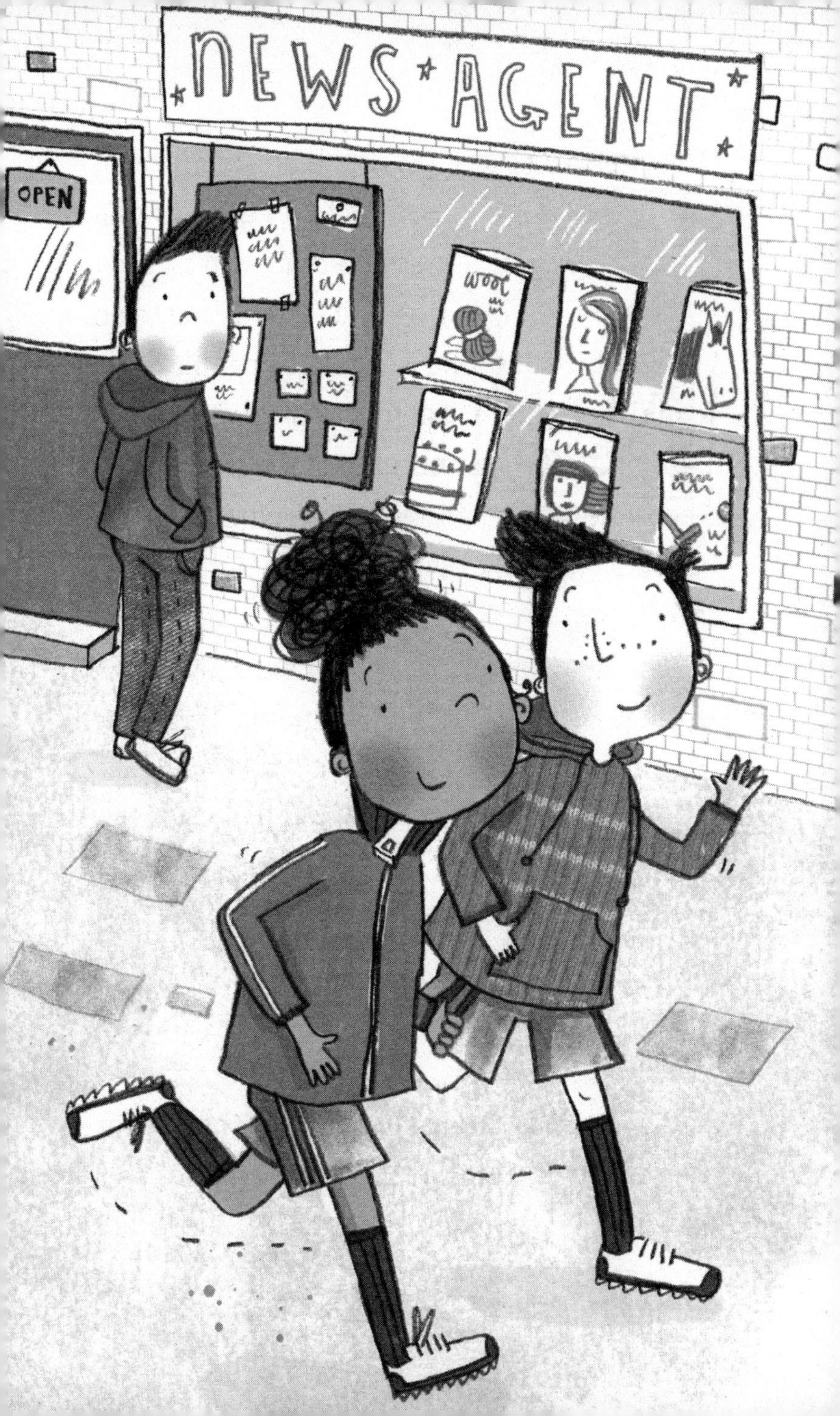
NEWS AGENT
OPEN
wool

they're training together blah blah blah. She went on and on about times and stuff till Phoebe yawned rather pointedly.

Phoebe said, 'Erika, he, this Ashley, he couldn't be the one who's threatening you, could he?' But Erika said, 'Thought of that and no. First he's nice; second we're both in the same team and want to win; third he was friendly to Rolly. Besides, all that's stopped now.'

'For the moment,' said Phoebe. 'And, this Ashley, he could just be pretending to be nice as a cover.'

Then Phoebe told Erika about Callum. 'He's following you round like a dog. It's creepy.'

But Erika just shrugged. 'He's probably just one of my fan-club.'

Honestly, I can see why she drives Phoebe mad sometimes.

But if Erika's not going to look out for herself we've got to look out for her.

Monday

Phoebe

In the playground this morning Daisy asked Callum straight out what he was up to. He said, 'Dunno what you mean,' and went bright red.

Then Erika breezed over. 'Leave him alone, you two!' Next thing she was chatting away to him about this Ashley and how great he was and how Saturday morning training had gone really well and how she and Ashley had improved their times. Blah blah.

YAWN!

Daisy went over to the infants' playground to sort out two little kids who were fighting, and I went to the loo.

When we were back in class Erika came and wrapped her arms round our shoulders. 'Thanks for trying to help, you guys, but – how many times do I have to tell you? – there's no need.' She whispered, 'No you-know-whats for days now, and – mystery solved – Callum is Ashley's cousin.'

She said she'd told Ashley about Callum, and he said it wasn't *her* Callum was following, but *him*. He was really embarrassed and said Callum had always sort of hero-worshipped him.

She obviously thought she'd explained away everything, but she didn't see what I saw a few minutes later.

Daisy

Phoebe says Callum was texting in class. Well, she saw his hand in his pocket. I said, 'So? That doesn't prove anything.' She said he got one back almost immediately. She heard it *ping*. I said that still doesn't prove anything. She said, 'It must have been important for him to text in class and risk getting his phone confiscated.'

At packed lunches we asked Erika if she'd had any texts and she rolled her eyes. 'NO, because one – we're not allowed to have our mobiles on in class, remember, and two – I told you, that's all stopped!' She showed us her empty inbox.

Then I asked her what she'd talked to Callum about when we'd gone and she said, 'Stuff that wouldn't interest you two. Sporty stuff.'

I said, 'I'm interested. It's Phoebe who isn't.'

Erika sighed dramatically then said, 'Mainly Ashley, if you must know, and how his dad will give him a hard time if he doesn't win. He said if he's beaten by a girl he'll never hear the end of it.'

Phoebe said '*Mmm*' and nodded as if she'd spotted an important clue, which made Erika snort. 'It's not what you're thinking. Ashley wouldn't threaten Rolly. '

Phoebe said, 'I was only going to say Callum's trying to make you feel sorry for Ashley, to slow you down.'

'Slow me down?' Erika looked at her as if she was mad.

But when Erika rang me after school she was HYSTERICAL.

Erika

ROLLY HAS GONE!!!!

When I got home from school he wasn't there. We walked in – Mum, me and my two brothers – and the house was very quiet, which was unusual. Rolly usually starts throwing himself at the door when he hears us. Well, at first I thought he must be in the garden because Mum leaves him there sometimes when she comes to pick me up from school, but when I went outside he wasn't there!

I started to worry. Then I thought Dad had taken him for a walk till I realised Dad's car wasn't there. Then I yelled, 'Mum, Rolly's gone!' in total panic and she yelled back, 'He must have escaped again!'

Well, he did have a phase of getting out of the garden when he was smaller and before Dad put up wire netting behind the hedge. Mum came out to the garden, but she seemed more annoyed than worried and said we'd look for him later, when she'd got the tea in the oven. But she doesn't know what I know, so I rang Dais.

Next thing Dais is banging on the door. She'd whizzed round on her bike and went straight into detective mode. It must be all those books she reads. Soon we're in the back garden on our hands and knees examining the hedge at the back. Dais found the hole. Someone had cut through the wire netting.

It was obvious, though they'd tried to pull the edges together to cover the gap.

'They must have had wire clippers,' said Daisy. 'You have to be quite strong to make them work. And they've broken some branches so I think this is the work of a grown-up or a strong teenager.'

I found some of Rolly's lovely woolly hair clinging to the broken branches as if he'd been dragged through and have to admit I started crying. By this time I was frantic. Mum must have been watching through the kitchen

window because she came out and when she saw the hole she zoomed into action. Well, after she'd got the boys back in the garden. They'd charged through the hole onto the road at the back. Mum rang the police straightaway. I thought they'd zoom round in a police car but they didn't.

We waited and waited but they didn't come. Mum said lost dogs – even stolen dogs – aren't a priority for the hard-pressed police force, especially if the dog isn't a pedigree. She said, 'Rolly isn't valuable, Erika.'

I said, 'He is to me! He's priceless!'

Then I blurted out about the threats and everything and she rang the police again. Mum says I mustn't let this affect my performance, to leave it to her, she'll sort it, but I've decided what I'm going to do. NOT do. I'm NOT going to run and I'm going to make sure everyone knows. All I want to do is get Rolly back.

Tuesday

Phoebe

I feel really sorry for Erika. She's frantic. She really does love Rolly more than she loves winning. I sometimes had my doubts about that, but Daisy says she knew all along that Erika had a heart. She just doesn't show it sometimes.

I think the only reason Erika came to school today was to tell everyone she wasn't going to run in the Three Counties Final. Her eyes were all red from crying. She said she'd texted everyone she could in the Athletics Club too. In the dinner hour we made loads of LOST DOG notices, offering a big reward to the finder. Miss Perkins let us stay in. Erika says she's going to put her bike on eBay to get the money. Daisy and I are doing everything we can to help. We're all going to put the notices up after school.

Trouble is some people are making Erika feel worse. She got loads of texts back from people in the Athletics Club saying she has to think of the team not herself. But she's not thinking of herself, she's thinking of Rolly.

Even Mrs Davies says she thinks Erika should run, and of course her mum does. They both say it's wrong to give in to blackmailers because it encourages them.

Mrs Davies gave an assembly about it and said that anybody who knew anything about Rolly should go and tell her. I watched Callum who looked at his feet all the time. I'm sure he knows something. I mean *who is he texting and who's texting him?*

I want to follow him home tonight – and see if he meets anyone. He might even lead us to Rolly. We could do it because Erika's mum has invited us to tea and to Athletics Club afterwards. Erika doesn't want to go, but her mum says she's got to. And Daisy has persuaded Erika to go – she said we might get more clues – so Erika's mum thinks we're on her side.

Daisy

Callum walked home – well as far as Erika's – with us, so Phoebe's plan was scuppered. But she's still convinced Callum's trying to put Erika off running because he wants Ashley to win. She also thinks he knows something about the Rolly-napping, but he sounded all sympathetic when we talked about it, and said he hoped she'd find Rolly at home when she got there.

I'm not sure.

Rolly wasn't at home. Callum came in with us and Erika showed him the hole in the hedge. Poor Erika looks awful, as if she hasn't slept since Rolly went, but I'd be the same if it was Marmalade.

When Callum left, Phoebe waited a few seconds then shot off after him. I knew she was going to follow him – to see if he led her

153

to Rolly – but I thought it would look odd if we both went so I said let's examine the hole again.

Erika and I climbed through easily, so I'm convinced it was someone tall. In the lane at the back I noticed tyre marks in the mud at the side, as if a car was parked there recently. So we're probably looking for someone who can drive.

Phoebe came back while I was trying to work out how to take a photo of the tyre marks on my mobile.

Phoebe

Daisy's very excited about the tyre marks, but what does she want us to do? Go round examining car tyres? Matching them up? There could be thousands of cars with tyres like that. I said, 'Daisy, you're not Miss Marple.'

'Have you got a better idea?' she asked.

Trouble is, I haven't.

The Callum trail led nowhere, well only to his house, so before he went in I came out of hiding and asked him straight out, 'Where's Rolly?' He made that screw loose sign and said, 'How do I know?' I said, 'There's no need to be rude, Callum, I know you're trying to put Erika off so that Ashley beats her. That isn't fair, you know.'

He went red then, but shouted, 'I don't know where her daft mutt is! If I knew I'd tell you!'

I don't know if I believe him.

Erika is hoping Rolly will just turn up now she's said she's not running. She thinks the dognappers will let him go.

Daisy said, 'Sorry, Erika, but I don't think they will let him go just because you've *said* you won't run. They'll wait till after the race and see if you keep your word.'

'But that's a whole week away!' Erika started crying again.

Erika

Rolly hates being away from home unless I'm with him, or at least someone in our family is. When we go away on holiday my gran comes to stay with him. We put him in kennels once, just for a weekend, and he refused to eat. What if he hasn't eaten for days? He could pine away completely!

Another thing, Mum says I've got to go to the track tonight. Well, I'll go but I'm NOT running. I don't care what she or anyone says. If someone's spying they'll see I'm not running. I know I'm giving in to blackmail, but what else can I do?

wednesday

Daisy

Last night at the track I was really proud of Erika. She refused to run even though her mum was furious. Several people came up and said, 'Think of the team' and stuff like that but Erika wouldn't give in.

Ashley looked miserable. He ran round the track but as if he had heavy weights tied to his feet. When he came in nearly last his dad looked as if he might hit him, but this girl with a scary haircut and nose-ring – I'd say she was about sixteen – said, 'Cool it, Dad. He hasn't recovered his form yet, that's all.'

But that wasn't all. At school today Callum said to Erika that Ashley had told his dad that he wouldn't run if Erika didn't, and his dad went ballistic and locked him in his room.

Erika said, 'Tell him to run. Tell him I said so. I don't want him getting into trouble on my behalf.' And Callum said, 'Thanks, Erika, that's what we hoped you'd say, but can you sort of put it in writing so he knows?'

Phoebe put her face really close to his and said, 'We? You said "That's what *we* hoped you'd say." So who's putting you up to this? Who's "we"?'

Callum went red then and said, 'Er, Ashley and me, of course.'

Phoebe said, 'I don't believe you. You'd better tell us the truth, Callum, or I'm going to tell everyone you've got a crush on Erika. Everyone's noticed you've been following her around.'

It was a brilliant tactic. Callum spilled straightaway. 'Lynne, Ashley's big sister. It's just because she's worried about him.'

Neither of us asked if she'd been sending the threatening texts, or more importantly, if she'd dognapped Rolly but we're pretty sure it must be her.

At break Erika wrote a note to Ashley and gave it to Callum.

Phoebe and I think we're getting warm, but what do we do next?

Erika

Ashley's just phoned to say thanks for the note but he still doesn't want to run, because he THINKS HIS SISTER LYNNE HAS BEEN SENDING ME THREATENING TEXTS!

He heard her talking to her boyfriend about it. He said not to blame her because he's sure she was trying to help. And she's always looked out for him since his mum died. But then his phone went all funny and I couldn't hear anything. Oh, poor Ashley, I didn't know he hadn't got a mum. But that doesn't help me find Rolly. Or does it?

I rang straight back to say ASK HER WHERE ROLLY IS!!! But there was no answer. His phone must have run out of battery.

I really really want to go straight round his house but I'm feeling awful. I don't know if it's because I'm frantic with worry about Rolly or I've got that bug Ashley had. Probably both. Oh no, I've got to go to the loo again!

I know what I'll do – text Daisy.

Thursday

Phoebe

We're on the trail!

Erika's not at school today, but she phoned Daisy this morning begging us both to help find Rolly because she was feeling too ill. Seems she can't risk not being near a toilet. *I* think we should go the police now we've got more evidence, but Daisy's gone into Miss Marple mode – triple! She's taken a photo of the tyre-track prints and says we should go round Ashley's house, and see if there's a car outside. If there is and if the tyre marks match we should wait till someone gets in it and follow them.

I asked her, 'HOW, Daisy? On our bikes?'

She said, 'Well at least we can find out which direction they're going in.'

I was about to say, 'OK then,' when someone yelled, 'It's snowing!' and everyone rushed to the window including Miss Perkins. It's not fair. We should be thinking about building a snowman after school or having a snowball fight, not looking for horrible dognappers. But we've got to try. Rolly's been missing for four days now and if he hasn't been eating . . . It's too awful to think about.

Anyway, I have agreed to go with Daisy to Ashley's house after school so Daisy can try her matching tyre marks idea – if there's a car outside – but first I've got to get Callum to tell me Ashley's address.

I feel a bit bad because we've told our mums we're going to take a get well-card to Erika. Still, if we do that afterwards it won't be a fib and we might have some good news about Rolly.

Daisy

Phoebe got Ashley's address from Callum easy-peasy, along with desperate pleas not to drop him in it. She said Callum seemed dead scared of Ashley's big sister, so we approached the house warily.

It took us about ten minutes to get there. Number 22 Meadway is an oldish house on an estate and it looks a bit scruffy. Luckily, though, it's on a corner and there's a hedge in front of it so we had two places to hide. But there wasn't a car outside. Phoebe wanted to leave right then, but I persuaded her to wait a bit, to see if a car would come. Then something even better happened!

First we saw Ashley looking out of an upstairs window, and he saw us and started waving, no not waving I realised at last, but pointing – downwards.

Then we saw why – the front door opened and his sister came out carrying a plastic bag that looked quite heavy though not very full. A tin of dog food? Possibly, from the way it thumped against her leg.

Well, we scooted round the corner to hide and watch. Which direction would she go in? Oh no! Towards the road we were hiding in! But we got behind a post-box just before she walked right past the end of the road. Then we set off after her, hoping she wouldn't turn round. Mind you, we had our hoods pulled up and our heads down.

Lynne strode along as if she knew where she was going. After about five minutes we saw a primary school, St Asaph's – Erika had told us that's where Ashley goes – and then some allotments surrounded by railings. Lynne slowed down and Phoebe touched my arm and I knew what she was thinking because I had the same thought.

There were sheds dotted all over the allotments. Rolly could be in one of them. There weren't many people about. In fact the allotments were deserted as they must have been all winter. I was thinking that no one would have heard poor Rolly if he had been howling when Phoebe's grip tightened.

Lynne had stopped at a gate.

We stopped and pressed ourselves against the railings.

Lynne looked round then opened the gate.

Our plan was to stay out of sight and watch, just watch and find out where Rolly was so we could rescue him later.

But our plan went wrong.

Phoebe

We were pressed against the railings when a car drew up and a HUGE teenager got out!

He yelled, 'Lynne!'

She turned round still holding the gate and the giant teenager started coming towards US. 'D'ya know these two scags?'

Well, of course we ran, and Daisy got away, but he grabbed hold of my arm.

'What two?' Lynne came running up. 'What are you doing, idiot? Let her go.'

'This girl, these girls . . . they were spying on you. They've been following you. Look.' He pointed to our footprints in the snow.

I said, 'We were coming to the allotments. That's all.' I looked round desperately though I hoped that didn't show. 'To pick some Brussel sprouts for our mum.'

Brussel sprouts were about the only things I could see growing.

Lynne stared at me. 'Do I know you?'

I shrugged and shook my head and hoped she didn't recognise me from my one visit to the track.

'What about the other one?' said Giant Teenager.

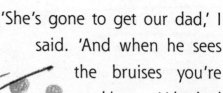

'She's gone to get our dad,' I said. 'And when he sees the bruises you're making . . .' I looked pointedly at his tattooed fingers still gripping my arm.

Lynne said, 'I told you to let her go. Come *on*.' She was standing by the car. 'Come ON!'

Reluctantly he let go. Then they both got into the car. They both swore when it didn't start straightaway and I held my breath. I was shaking. It seemed ages before the car spluttered into action and they roared off in a cloud of exhaust smoke.

Now what? It was beginning to get dark, snow was falling again and the place was deserted. *Should I start searching the huts all by myself for Rolly or try and find my way home?*

Daisy

Phoebe didn't know that I was watching. I was hiding in the school yard texting and phoning desperately. Trouble is I didn't get any answers. No one replied. So much for having mobiles to use in emergencies!

As soon as the car roared off I came out of hiding and yelled, 'Phoebe!' I made my way as fast as I could to her, slipping and sliding on the snowy path.

'What happened?' I gasped. 'How did you get rid of them? You were brilliant!'

Phoebe looked as if she was going to cry. 'Rolly, I'm sure he's in one of those sheds.'

I nodded, I could tell Phoebe was longing to go home and I didn't blame her – she must have been terrified. But I said, 'He could be starving, Phoebe. We've got to get him *now*.'

She nodded again, she was so brave, and

I could tell she was thinking, what if Lynne and her giant boyfriend come back? But she said, 'Let's call his name and see if he answers.'

'Rolly! Rolly!' My voice came out high and squeaky, I was so scared, but I think dogs can hear high-pitched sounds better.

But he didn't seem to hear me. Well, he didn't respond. All we could hear was the wind sighing in some far off trees.

I tried calling again.

Still nothing, or – could that sighing sound be a dog whimpering?

We listened again and I thought I heard a yelp.

So did Phoebe. 'Over there! In the corner!'

Phoebe

We charged over the frozen allotment plots to the far corner and as we got nearer the yelps got louder.

'That one!' we gasped together, pointing to a shack made of wooden crates and sheets of corrugated iron. Daisy tried wrenching open the door but it was stronger than it looked – and padlocked!

Rolly was going frantic on the other side.

We tried to comfort him.

'Don't worry, boy. We'll get you out.'

But how?

I pointed at the door hinges, which looked as if they were made of leather. Daisy spotted a spade in one of the plots.

'Out of the way, Rolly! Stand back!'

Between us we managed to hack through one of the hinges, then bend back the door and . . . there was Rolly trembling with joy!

Erika

I couldn't believe it when I heard Daisy shouting below my bedroom window.

'We've found him! We've found him!'

And they hadn't just found him, they'd got him. I looked out of my window and there he was in their arms. My two friends are the bestest friends in the world, and I don't care if Miss Perkins says you can't say bestest. They'd carried Rolly all the way home from these allotments where he'd been hidden, because his paws were so sore he couldn't walk. He must have been trying to escape for days.

Poor Rolly, but he's on the mend now and so am I.

And Rolly's not the only prisoner who's been set free. Ashley is too and his life has changed quite a lot – for the better, I'm glad to say.

In the end the police did find time to investigate and they went round Ashley's house to warn Lynne and her boyfriend that if they ever did anything like that again they'd be in serious trouble. Ashley says Lynne broke down and said she was only trying to help, and then to Ashley's amazement his dad said it was his fault. *His* – I mean – *his dad's*! He actually apologised for putting Ashley under too much pressure.

You may have noticed that I haven't mentioned the Three Counties race. That's because it didn't happen – it was snowed off – but when it's on again Ashley and I are both going to do our very best to win, cheered on by all our friends.

AND, as I've got a few extra days, and can't train anyway, I've agreed to be Magpie in the play.

It's the least I can do for Dais and Phoebe who are THE BEST!

New friend
Old Friends

To Faith, Maya, Lois and Ursula, my sparky granddaughters.

Acknowledgements

Huge thanks to Sajida Raza of Sythwood Primary School, who thought of the title and helped a lot; to Seherish Ahmed, who showed me how to write 'welcome' in Urdu; to the pupils of Grove Road Primary School, who advised me on how a *shalwar kameez* is worn; and to Vimla Randhawa, librarian at Redbourne Upper School, who checked the script for howlers.

Tuesday

Phoebe

Mrs Davies has chosen *me* to look after the new girl!

I thought she'd choose Daisy because she's a school buddy. Or Erika because she's on the school council. But she chose *me*! I suppose she thought Daisy had enough to do looking out for bullies, and Erika's always busy doing sporty stuff.

The new girl's name is Shazia. I haven't met her yet – she starts on Monday. But I've already been thinking about how I'm going to help her. Mrs Davies says she comes from Pakistan and may not speak much English so I'm going to try and learn some words from her language to help her feel at home. That's *my* idea. I'll find out how to say 'Hello' and 'Welcome to our school.'

Then I'll teach everyone else!

I haven't told Daisy and Erika yet, even though they're my best friends. I'm not sure why I didn't let them know today at school really, but when Mrs Davies told me it felt, well, like a really exciting secret. But she didn't say it was a secret – and they'll be miffed if I don't tell them – so I'll text them both now:

GOT EXCITING NEWS!!! COME ROUND!

I can't stop thinking about it. I mean, I'll have to show Shazia where everything is and make sure she's not lonely and take her to dinners and everything!

Shazia. Sounds like a princess in a fairytale!

Daisy

Phoebe had something really exciting to tell us – a new girl from Pakistan is starting at school. That's near India. Phoebe got out a map and showed us. Mrs Davies has asked her to be the new girl's special buddy and she's taking her job very seriously. *Shazia!* What a lovely name! I'm *so* looking forward to meeting her. I wonder what she'll be like. Phoebe didn't know much about her, but I hope she'll find out. Phoebe can be rather shy and so might not ask many questions. I wonder what sort of clothes Shazia will wear. Oh, boring thought – she'll probably wear school uniform like everyone else.

Whatever she's like, we'll *all* have to do everything we can to make her feel at home. Actually – I didn't say this to Phoebe – but I'm surprised Mrs Davies didn't ask *me* to look after Shazia. I mean, I'm the one who's a buddy. Anyway I can give Phoebe lots of tips. I'll lend her my *How to Be a Buddy* handbook. And I can teach Shazia playground games and explain about the buddy seat, where anyone can sit if they're feeling lonely.

And – I know! – I'll get Mum to invite her round for some of her Asian cooking! Mum travelled round India and Pakistan when she was a student and picked up some recipes.

I rushed home after Phoebe told us her news and Mum's taught me some Pakistani words already, well Urdu. That's the name of the language they speak, though Mum says they have lots of languages. Just hope it's the right one.

'Hello' is *'Aslam-U-Alaikum'*, 'Yes' is *'Jee'* and 'No' is *'Naheen'*. Sounds quite easy! But that's because they're written down in English the way they *sound*. When they're written down like they would be in Pakistan they use a completely different alphabet.

I'll text them all to Phoebe. Mum says she's sure Shazia will speak good English because in most schools in Pakistan lessons are taught in English.

I wonder if Shazia has brothers and sisters, or whether she's an only child like me.

Erika

Phoebe's news is cool. It'll be great to have another girl in our class. We're outnumbered by the boys at the mo. Hope she's sporty. We're short of players for most of our teams. Mum says Pakistan is famous for cricket and hockey, but she thought only men played sport there.

But she's wrong!

I just Googled Pakistani sports women and they've got a great hockey team and they do squash and gymnastics. In fact a girl called Shazia won a gold medal for gymnastics when she was only eight. Can't be the same Shazia, worse luck, because that was ages ago. Wish it was though. That would be really cool.

It's a pity we don't play hockey at our school – but we will when we go up to seniors – and I'm sure *our* Shazia will want to learn how to play rounders and netball and even five-a-side. I'll teach her the rules. And she can join gym club.

I can't wait to meet her. I hope she speaks English.

Why did Phoebe wait till tonight to tell us? If it had been Daisy or me with news like that we'd have been bursting to tell. She's very secretive sometimes.

wednesday

Phoebe

Shazia came to school this afternoon and she seems really nice and friendly! It was just for a visit though. She isn't starting school till Monday. She was with her mum and her sister and two little brothers who were ever so naughty! Just like my little brothers!

Our head teacher, Mrs Davies, brought them into our classroom when we were doing art. At first I thought Shazia was the eldest, because she's the tallest, but she isn't. Her sister's going to the senior school. Her brothers are only toddlers, a bit older than the Smellies – that's what I call my little brothers – and they were even more badly behaved than mine!

I couldn't believe it. They chased each other round the classroom, knocking paint pots over, and their mum didn't do *anything*

192

except look really upset. I think she was worried about her lovely clothes. There was paint flying everywhere. When Shazia and her sister tried to catch the boys they dived under the table in the writing corner and wouldn't come out. Well, not till after Mrs Davies had quickly opened the door and said, 'We'll go and see the library now.'

Even then they waited till their mum was out of sight in the corridor.

Miss Perkins almost slammed the door shut when they'd gone, but it opened again and there was Shazia. She went straight up to Miss Perkins's desk and said, 'I am sincerely sorry about my little brothers. I call them the Monsters and I faithfully promise never ever to bring them to school again.'

Then she walked away with her head bowed – till she reached the door when she turned and gave us all a little wave. I think I managed to catch her eye and give her an encouraging smile – and a wave – because she smiled back, but that may have been to everyone.

I'm longing to tell her about the Smellies and that I completely understand how she feels.

I just wish someone had told me she was coming in today. And it would have been nice if Mrs Davies or Miss Perkins had told Shazia and everyone that it's *my* job to look after her.

Daisy's being very pushy. She managed to say something to Shazia but I don't know what.

And afterwards she told everyone how to say 'Welcome' in Urdu and that was *my* idea!

Daisy

Shazia's going to be really good fun!

Mum was right – she already speaks English so I don't think I'm going to have to use my Urdu. I managed to say *'Kush-amdeed'* though when she shot past my desk trying to catch her little brothers and I think she was pleased.

'Kush-amdeed' means welcome.

Shazia wore really nice clothes – baggy trousers, a long-sleeved tunic top and a scarf. Mum says the outfit's called *shalwar kameez*. It was turquoise and silver and silky and it went really well with her dark hair and skin. And her sandals were silver too. Mind you they had a few red and yellow spots on them when she'd finished chasing after her brothers.

Her mum and sister were dressed in gorgeous clothes too. Her mum had this

gauzy scarf round her shoulders. It had floaty ends with beads on them. I didn't notice what her brothers wore. They spent most of their time under the writing table.

Hope Shazia will do clothes swaps! That would be awesome.

I wonder where they live. I've been keeping a lookout for new people moving in round here, but haven't spotted any removal vans.

Erika

Shazia lives at *my* end of the village!

I saw her going into the flats with her family, all of them even her dad. I rushed out to tell her I lived near and invite her round mine, but by the time I got inside the flats the whole family had disappeared into the lift.

Wish I knew which flat they'd moved in to, or what her surname was. Then I could write her a note and leave it in one of the little post boxes in the entrance.

I'm going to ask her if she'd like to come for a run with me and Rolly. He's my wumply dumply dog. It's light in the evenings now that spring is here and I want to run as much as I can.

I know, I'll text Phoebe and ask her what Shazia's full name is. Hope she knows.

Shazia looked really agile running between the desks when she was trying to catch her little brothers. Pity about the long trousers and sandals though. If she'd been wearing shorts and a pair of trainers she'd have caught those boys easy peasy.

'We'll have to get her kitted out, won't we, Rolly?'

Oh, I hope she likes dogs.

Phoebe

I don't know Shazia's last name and I wouldn't tell Erika if I did. Oh! Why did I say that? It makes me feel mean. I really do want *everyone* to be friendly to Shazia. It would be awful if they weren't, but . . .

It's just that if Erika gets Shazia doing all that sporty stuff . . . well, she won't have any time left for doing stuff with me and Daisy.

I wish Shazia was living at *our* end of the village – mine and Daisy's – so she could come round our houses and do arty crafty things or Moshi Monsters.

Though, actually, even Daisy's going on as if *she* was Shazia's special buddy. She says her mum is going to invite Shazia round for chapattis, or something. I asked Mum if I could invite Shazia round and she said, 'Not this week, Phoebe! Don't you think I've got enough to do?'

It's because the Smellies are being really difficult at the moment.

Oh. Here's a text from Daisy:

LET'S INVITE SHAZIA FOR A CLOTHES SWAP!

Nice idea, but . . .

There I go again. But it would have to be round Daisy's house, wouldn't it? And I think it's a bit soon for that sort of thing anyway. I mean – will Shazia want to rush round Daisy's house and start trying on our things? I wouldn't want to if I'd just started at a new school.

I'm fed up with Daisy being bossy. *'You must do this, Phoebe. You must do that.'*

Miss Perkins *still* hasn't told everyone that Mrs Davies asked *me* to look after Shazia.

Daisy

Phoebe's in one of her moods.

I just went round to hers because she hadn't answered my text and her mum said she'd gone to bed early because she was tired. I don't believe her, that she's tired I mean. Phoebe's a night owl. When we have sleepovers she's always the last to go to sleep. She may be in her bedroom, even in bed, but I bet she's not asleep. It's far too early and the Smellies were still running around making a terrible racket.

So what's bugging her?

I can't think of anything I've done. I mean, I've been doing everything I can to *help* her with the new girl.

Oh. Here's a text from Erika.

NEED NEW GIRL'S FULL NAME. PHOEBE NOT ANSWERING. STROP?

Mmm. So Phoebe's not answering Erika, either. But Phoebe doesn't strop. She droops.

I wonder why Erika wants Shazia's full name.

I'm texting Phoebe again.

WHAT'S THE MATTER? TELL ME!

Thursday

Erika

Phoebe *is* in a strop, whatever Daisy says. Well, she *was* for most of the morning. When I got to school and asked her what Shazia's surname was again, she blanked me. She pretended she hadn't heard, but I'm sure she had.

Daisy said Phoebe hardly spoke at all on the way to school and she disappeared at break.

That *is* a strop.

Luckily she cheered up after break, but only when Miss Perkins said, 'Let's have a little chat about the new girl, Shazia, shall we? I know you'll all make her very welcome but, just to make sure she's never left on her own, Mrs Davies has asked Phoebe to be her special buddy for the first few days.'

Phoebe smiled for the first time that day. I think she asked Miss Perkins to say that.

Then Miss Perkins said, 'Let's find out what we can about where Shazia comes from, shall we?'

She got the globe and pointed to a country on the other side of the world.

'Shazia and her family have come all the way from Pakistan which is a country in Asia. She lived in a busy town called Karachi. That's by the sea so she's going to find our village very different.'

She switched on the whiteboard and Googled some photographs of Karachi. It looked VERY different from our village. There was an amazing mix of buildings – high-rise flats and mosques with golden domes, little white flat-roofed houses and towers you could hide Rapunzel in. The traffic was a mix too – huge lorries and little carts pulled by donkeys, swanky cars with dark windows and decorated camels, all jumbled up together with people weaving in and out.

Afterwards I went and asked Miss Perkins if she knew Shazia's family name and she did! It was already in the register.

Her name is Shazia Majeed.

Phoebe

Shazia came into school today – *with Erika!*

When Daisy and I entered the playground Shazia was there, though at first we didn't notice. We just saw Erika with the sporty crowd round her which is quite normal. Then they all drifted across the playground to the netball post and, next thing, Erika was shouting, 'Well done, Shazia!'

And there she was! She'd just scored a goal. We hadn't noticed her at first because she was wearing school uniform just like everyone else, except that she wore trousers, not a pleated skirt like the rest of the girls.

I was so shocked! I didn't know why she was in school today. Why had nobody told me? *I'm* her special buddy.

Daisy said, 'Come on. Let's go and watch

– or join in. It's not a match or anything. They're just practising shooting at goal.'

But I didn't feel like it.

Erika and Shazia already looked like best friends. It just wasn't fair. I'd been so excited about meeting Shazia and introducing her to everyone, and Erika had somehow got there first.

But all I said was, 'What are we going to do with our welcome signs?'

We'd made them the night before. Daisy's mum had helped us with the writing. They looked great. But we were going to make more at the weekend.

And we'd practised saying, 'Kush-amdeed.'

Daisy said, 'Let's go into school straight away and put them up just like we planned. I'm sure Mrs Davies will let us.'

I said, 'We can't do *as we planned*, Daisy, because we haven't got enough.' We wanted to put them all over the school.

Anyway, we got permission to go in before the bell and put them up in the classroom. We stuck one on the door so Shazia would see it when she came in, another above the whiteboard so she'd always see it when she was looking at the board and a third in the middle of our table.

Daisy, Erika and I are sitting together this term and there was a spare chair because the girl who used to sit there had left.

I'm beginning to think that's the only reason Mrs Davies chose me – because there's a space.

Anyway, Daisy and I sat down on opposite sides – that was my idea – so that there was an empty seat by each of us.

At least that way Shazia couldn't sit next to Erika.

But she sat next to Daisy, opposite Erika. So they were face to face which was worse. They talked non-stop and they told us that Erika had been round Shazia's house last night and convinced her to start school today!

Shazia did notice the welcome signs and said they were great but that was the only good thing.

Daisy

Phoebe's gone all droopy because she thinks Erika's taking over and trying to be Shazia's special buddy. That's what is bugging Phoebe. But I don't think Erika is. It's just that Erika wants everyone to join in – especially with games and sporty stuff. Erika wouldn't want to do things like show Shazia where to put her coat or where the toilets are.

At lunchtime today I told Shazia that I liked her clothes – the ones she wore when she visited the school. I asked her if she'd like to come round my house and do a clothes swap.

'Clothes swap? What does that mean?'

So I explained how Phoebe and I try on each other's clothes and sometimes borrow them for a while. 'But not school uniform,' I added quickly, thinking of her sparkly turquoise *shalwar kameez*.

Shazia giggled and shook her head and said, 'Sorry, Daisy. My parents would not allow.'

Erika said, 'Why on earth not?' Not that Erika is into swapping, well only trainers and tracksuits and sporty stuff.

Shazia blushed and didn't say anything till Phoebe said, 'It's about . . . *modesty*, isn't it, Shazia? Your parents wouldn't like you undressing in front of other people.'

Actually Phoebe perked up after that. Because she'd guessed right, I suppose. Anyway, she showed Shazia the drawer where she could keep her books and she helped her with her adverbs in literacy.

But at break Erika grabbed Shazia's arm and said, 'Come on, let's practise. I think you could be a really good goal attack.'

So Phoebe drooped again.

Actually, I felt a bit droopy too. I wanted to show Shazia my Moshi Monster cards.

Monday

netball

Phoebe

Erika says I've *got* to do something! Just because Shazia wasn't allowed out to play on Saturday! Erika told me she went round to Shazia's on Saturday morning to ask her to come and practise netball, but Shazia's dad wouldn't let her go out. He said she had to stay in and help her mother.

I said, 'Erika, sometimes Mum won't let me go out if she wants help with the Smellies.'

'It's not *sometimes*, Phoebe,' Erika wailed. 'It's always! Her dad said so. Shazia can't stay after school to practise and she can't come out at the weekend. Ever! So she can't be in the team even though she's a brilliant player and we need her. You're supposed to be helping her settle in. Well, she won't, not if she can't *join in*, so go and tell Miss Perkins.'

Miss Perkins is not just our form teacher. She also runs the netball team.

Without waiting for me to reply, Erika shot off – probably to tell Miss Perkins herself.

Then Shazia turned up so I asked her about what Erika had said. To my surprise she seemed even more upset than Erika.

'I *want* to be in the team, Phoebe. I want that very much. I was in the team at my school in Karachi. But I can't.'

Shazia looked as if she was going to cry so I led her to the buddy seat in the playground, and after a deep breath she started to explain.

'In Karachi we lived in a big house with many servants.'

'Servants!' I didn't know anyone with servants.

She nodded. 'Ami-ji, my mother was very happy then and laughed a lot. She helped me and my sister with our homework. We went out to see friends. We had a driver to take us. Another servant looked after the boys. They were nice boys, really cute then. But, Ami-ji, she does not know how to look after little children . . . She's never had to before.'

Shazia's eyes filled with tears so I put my arm round her.

'Now . . .' Shazia continued, 'Ami-ji cries all the time and my brothers run round like racing cars. Hiba, my big sister, she tried to help at first, but now she cries too . . .'

It sounded even worse than my house.

Shazia went on to say it wasn't at all what they expected when they heard that they were coming to England. Mr Majeed said they would have lots of money because he was coming to a good job with International Electronics. He's a computer engineer.

'But it does not seem so much money now because things are so expensive in England. So we live in a tiny flat instead of a big house. We do not have servants and we have only one car.'

I said, 'We've only got one car, Shazia. Daisy's mum hasn't got even one.'

But she didn't seem to hear. She said, 'No aunties, uncles or grandmas, either.' She missed her grandma most of all. She called her Daadi-Ami.

'Daadi-Ami would know what to do,' she whispered. 'But I don't.'

And nor do I!

Daisy

Phoebe has asked me for help but I don't know what we can do except be kind to Shazia at school. I mean we can't get them a big house and servants like they had in Pakistan.

But I did have one idea.

I said, 'Phoebe, does your mum still take the Smellies to a toddlers' group in the community hall?'

She does and they love it. So does Phoebe's mum because she gets to chat with the other mums while the Smellies play on all the equipment. We went with them once and there was a climbing frame and loads of space to charge around. Phoebe's mum said it stopped her going mad.

'And they want more people to go,' said Phoebe, 'or it's going to close down.'

Toddlers' Group is on Tuesday and Thursday afternoons. Tomorrow's Tuesday!

We raced to Phoebe's house after school and persuaded her mum to write a note to Shazia's mum, inviting her to Toddlers' Group. Phoebe's mum even offered to take them and she gave us a leaflet about the group. Then we ran to Erika's to find out exactly where Shazia lived. And we all went round to deliver the note together.

Shazia was ever so pleased to see us. She said, 'Come in quickly' because she had to close the door to stop the Monsters running out.

Then we all trooped into the sitting room to give Shazia's mum the note, and Phoebe explained why we'd come really well. I was very proud of her.

But then Shazia's mum shook her head!

I couldn't believe it. It was so disappointing. There we were with a really helpful suggestion and she said, 'Naheen.' No!

But then Shazia's dad came home from work and Shazia showed him Phoebe's mum's note and the leaflet, and he said, 'I think this is a very good proposal, Raheela. The hand of friendship is being offered and you must accept. You must go.'

Talk about bossy!

Erika

We all high-fived when we got outside.

Phoebe and Dais were well pleased that their plan to help was working. But I still wasn't sure it would help me get a team together for the match against St Swithins. We really needed Shazia as goal attack.

Dais thought it might help in the long run. She said, 'If Shazia's mum cheers up and starts learning how to look after little kids, then Shazia might be allowed to come out a bit more.'

So it was Operation Cheer Up Shazia's Mum.

I'm going to ask my mum to invite her round for coffee or a cup of tea. Trouble is, Mum's so busy. Just hope she's got a day off work coming up soon.

At least Shazia can still practise in school time.

Phoebe

I have to admit it's great having Daisy and Erika to help. Erika's mostly helping so Shazia can be in the netball team, but I see now that would make Shazia ever so happy.

And Daisy's idea about Toddlers' Group was a brainwave. It went really well. Luckily yesterday was a nice spring day. Mum says they opened the doors of the community hall so there was even more space outside. The Monsters and the Smellies raced round on ride-ons. The Monsters were a bit wild at first, Mum says, but that's because they've been cooped up in a flat without a garden. There was only one panic, at the end, when they couldn't find the Monsters. But – after a lot of searching – they found them under the stage where the ride-ons are stored!

226

Afterwards Mum took them to the playing fields next to our school. We saw them when we came out, scrambling over the climbing frame like monkeys. Well, the boys were! Our mums were sitting on a bench chatting.

Mum says Shazia's mum seems rather sad – everything is new for her and she's a bit overwhelmed and lonely – but Mum thinks getting out of the house will help.

At school today Shazia said the Monsters nearly fell asleep over their supper last night *and* when they were put to bed they stayed there *and* they slept the whole night through. Her mum didn't shout or cry at breakfast and she says she's going to take the boys to Toddlers' Group tomorrow.

The other exciting bit of news today is that there's going to be an extra school disco. In assembly Mrs Davies said that we need to raise funds for new books for the library.

I just hope Shazia can come to the disco.

Daisy

Do hope Shazia will be allowed to come to the disco. I think there's a good chance if she isn't needed at home so much. Shazia says her dad is really strict, but he seemed really nice – bossy and serious but nice – and sensible! A bit like me really!

Well, he was sensible about Toddlers' Group.

I'm sure Shazia can persuade him to let her go – if Operation Cheer Up Shazia's Mum is a success. It's got to be. Idea! I'll get Mum to invite them all round for that meal she promised to cook. We can talk about the disco, and how important it is to raise money for new books.

And I'll show Shazia my disco dancing gear!

Monday

Phoebe

Daisy has blown it! She's undone all our good work!

Daisy got her mum to invite the Majeeds round on Saturday – good – but then she paraded in her disco gear – *bad*! She actually came downstairs in her short skirt and skimpy skinny top! I mean how could she be so stupid? I'd explained about modesty when Shazia said she couldn't do clothes swapping. I explained all about different cultures with different ideas of right and wrong. I told her bare shoulders and legs were out – or rather not out.

But she hasn't apologised!

She says that it was all going well with the grown-ups sitting round after the meal being chatty. Mr and Mrs Majeed were saying how delicious her mum's food was. Then her

mum started telling them about the PTA and fundraising. Hiba, Shazia's sister, was keeping an eye on the Monsters, so Daisy said, 'Let's go upstairs, Shazia. I'll show you my disco gear.'

Today at school I said, 'Shazia, why didn't you stop Daisy going downstairs to show your parents?'

She said, 'I was in her home, Phoebe, and in her home she is doing what she wants to do. And my parents too they think people in their own homes do – how do you say? – do their "own thing".'

'But they went very quiet Daisy says.' Daisy *had* noticed that.

Shazia said, 'Yes, they were shocked, but they didn't say anything. That would be very impolite.'

'But they went home soon afterwards.'

'Only because they needed to put my brothers to bed.'

'But they won't let you go to the disco now.'
I felt sure.

But Shazia wasn't sure. 'I have not asked them yet. I am waiting for the right time. Life is better now that your mother has befriended my mother. I think they will let me go, if I wear my own clothes. I am . . . working on it.'

Then she giggled. 'Phoebe, I *loved* Daisy's disco clothes. I *did* try them on you know.'

I was speechless. What if her parents had come upstairs?

Erika

Daisy is crazy!

I mean, did she really think Shazia's mum and dad would like her disco clothes?

And Phoebe is being very *pheeble*! She is sure there's nothing we can do to persuade Shazia's mum and dad to let her come out more. But I'm not giving up. Not yet. Not when, with a bit of effort, we can save the day. I'm sure we can.

Another thing, Phoebe says that Shazia's dad will never ever let her play in matches, because he'll never ever let her wear shorts. But she doesn't have to! I've noticed that some teams play in tracksuit bottoms. So Shazia could too!

I'm going to ask Miss Perkins and I'm sure she'll agree. I mean, Shazia wears trousers for school anyway. In fact – just thought of this –

I'm going to put it to the school council that all girls can wear trousers if they want to. I mean, it's all right at the mo, but in winter our legs get freezing. Trousers would be much more sensible.

Two problems solved – well almost!

I'd better see Miss Perkins first thing tomorrow. In fact I'll ask her to phone Shazia's dad and try and persuade him to let her play in the match on Wednesday, wearing a tracksuit.

Daisy

Hooray!!

Shazia can go to the disco! And she can play in the match on Wednesday. Miss Perkins phoned her dad and persuaded him. Shazia told us all at school today. But only if she wears her *shalwar kameez*. For the disco not the match! Her father says she can't wear disco clothes and he has a special reason for wanting her to wear her traditional dress that night.

I said, 'That's fine, Shazia. Is it a special festival or something?'

Shazia said she didn't think it was, because if it was she'd have to stay at home and go to the mosque with her family.

I said, 'Really, Shazia, you'll look lovely.'

But she pulled a face. 'I've been thinking about it. I don't want to be the only one not wearing disco clothes. I want to look like you,

Daisy. I want to dance like you and everyone else and I cannot do that in a *shalwar kameez*. So this is my plan . . .'

She said she'd go to the disco in her traditional dress, and swap with me when she got there – because she knew how much I wanted to try on her *shalwar kameez*. Then we would change back again before the end, ready for when her mother or father met her.

I said, 'So I'd get to wear your *shalwar kameez*?'

'Only if you really want to, Daisy.'

I *do* want to, but, well, I wasn't sure about her plan. Was it too risky? What if we got caught?

I said, 'Your parents would be furious if they found out. They'd never trust you afterwards. You'd never ever be allowed out again. And they would be cross with me too.'

It would be the end of Operation Cheer Up Shazia's Mum for sure.

Shazia said, 'They won't find out. I will change back into my own clothes before the end of the disco.'

I said, 'Let's discuss this with Phoebe first – and Erika.'

Erika would be furious – with me! – if Shazia was grounded and couldn't play in her precious netball team. As for Phoebe, well, she'd never forgive me if I didn't tell her about this.

But Shazia didn't want me to tell them.

'Erika is – how do you say it? – a blabber mouth? She is sure to tell someone. And Phoebe, lovely Phoebe, it would worry her very much.'

'It worries *me* very much.'

Shazia laughed. 'No, you like adventures, Daisy.'

I said, 'In books, Shazia.'

She giggled and linked her arm in mine. 'We will be in *disguise*. It will be exciting.'

Shazia's so fun! And if she's willing to take the risk, shouldn't I be braver too? Suddenly it *seemed* very exciting. I pictured myself in her gorgeous *shalwar kameez* . . .

Shazia put her finger over her lips. 'This will be our secret, Daisy.'

Phoebe

Shazia isn't so chatty at the moment, not to me, except about netball and I don't care about stupid netball. I'm pleased she's going to play for the team today but I don't want to hear all about 'Wonderful Erika' arranging everything.

And Erika's going round as if she's won the lottery.

But Daisy's behaving even more strangely. She's been really odd all week. She's gone all quiet. I haven't had a proper goss with her for days. And we usually talk lots about what we're going to wear when there's a disco coming up. I know I had a go at her about last Saturday night but I'd have thought she'd have got over that by now.

If it were anyone else I'd assume they were

just in a mood. But Daisy doesn't have moods – well, not like I do. She can't bear to be on bad terms with anyone for long.

And she *is* talking to Shazia – a lot. I heard them talking about the disco, but they stopped when they saw me.

It's as if they're plotting something.

Daisy

I've changed my mind.

I've been trying to persuade Shazia not to go ahead with it, but she's determined. I've never met anyone so determined, well, except Erika when she's in a race. Perhaps that's why those two get on so well. And they get on even better now Shazia's in the netball team.

But Erika would *not* like Shazia's plan. Nor would Phoebe and I think she's getting suspicious. At break today she said, 'What are you going to wear for the disco, Shazia?'

The three of us were in the playground. Well, I held my breath, wondering what Shazia would say, when Erika breezed out on her way to the games area.

'Come on, Shazia. Let's practise!'

As the two of them ran off across the

playground Phoebe looked like a hurt kitten, then a suspicious kitten.

I said, 'Sporty types, eh?' I tried to laugh it off, but Phoebe looked at me with her eyes scrunched up.

'Do you know what Shazia is wearing for the disco, Daisy? Is that what you've been whispering about?'

Well, I felt myself going red. Honestly, I wanted to tell her. I was longing to talk it over with her, but I'd promised Shazia I wouldn't.

Sort of promised. I hadn't actually *said* I wouldn't. But Shazia thought I had.

Phoebe persisted. 'You know, don't you? She's up to something and you know what her plan is.'

Well, I didn't say anything, but my tummy was squirgling and all sorts of thoughts were going round in my head. *It was right to tell Phoebe. It was wrong. I'd upset Shazia if I did. Shazia might be in big trouble if I didn't.*

Phoebe was still staring at me.

I said, 'Can you keep a secret?'

Thursday

Erika

We won 5–0 yesterday and Shazia scored three of our goals!

Her dad picked us up after school and when we arrived at their flat her mum met us with garlands of flowers which she put round our necks. Her little brothers clapped. They were quite sweet in fact. I felt as if I'd won at the Olympics.

Tea was delicious, spicy but not too hot and I ate *loads*.

After tea her dad said, 'Why don't you show Erika your best *shalwar kameez* that you are wearing for the disco, Shazia? Go to your bedroom and put it on.'

When Shazia came back I didn't know what to say.

The outfit was my favourite colour, purple, and had silver and gold embroidery and matching slippers. Dais and Phoebe would have drooled and gasped, 'Gorgeous'. They love girlie things, the silkier and sparklier the better, but it wasn't really my style.

'Well, what are you thinking?' said Mr Majeed. 'Do you not think all the girls will want an outfit like that?'

I said, 'Yes. It's lovely. Daisy would swap like a shot if she had the chance.'

But mentioning Daisy obviously wasn't a good idea. Shazia's eyes opened wide and she shook her head frantically.

Mrs Majeed said, 'What will you be wearing for the disco, Erika?'

'Not sure yet,' I replied. It was true. I mean the disco wasn't till the weekend. I said, 'I've had more important things on my mind recently, like the match – and my school work.'

I could almost hear Daisy saying, 'Creep' as I said that, but it was exactly the right thing to say.

Mr Majeed thought I was great. 'You are very sensible, Erika. I am glad that Shazia has a sensible friend. I hope you will both enjoy the disco.'

Shazia said, 'I'm sure we will. Thank you, *Abu-ji.*'

She sounded like a really good little girl, but then she winked at me. *What* was that about?

Phoebe

I can't believe what Daisy and Shazia are planning to do on Saturday!

I said, 'Daisy, you can't. It's crazy.'

Then she said, 'I know. But . . .'

'But what?'

'Shazia's so keen to fit in and . . .'

'And?'

'And she's so excited about it and she trusts me. Please don't tell her I told you, Phoebe. I don't want to let her down. You know how unhappy she was before this and she's quite sure her parents won't find out and . . .'

'And?' I was still waiting for a really good reason.

Daisy sort of smiled. 'It could be really good fun, Phoebe. Please help us.'

'How?'

'By not breathing a word.'

Daisy explained how they were going to do the swap. 'Shazia will arrive in her *shalwar kameez*. I'll arrive in my disco gear. As soon as we're sure our parents have gone we'll dive into the toilets and change.'

I said, 'What about changing back, Daisy? Remember Cinderella? *Dong! Dong! Dong!* She forgot the time.'

'Good point,' she said. 'That's something you could do – keep an eye on the clock. If we swap back a good quarter of an hour before the end of the disco, we'll be in our own clothes well before the parents arrive to pick us up.'

I said, 'Half an hour would be better. What if they come early?'

'Another good point, Phoebe!' Daisy hugged me. 'I feel much better now you've agreed to help.'

I didn't realise I had!

Erika

The disco's tomorrow night and something's up.

Last week Dais and Phoebe weren't speaking. This week they've been whispering all the time. But they're not exactly best friends. At break today I heard Daisy snap, 'NO, Phoebe. How many times do I have to tell you?' But they wouldn't tell me what they were arguing about.

Daisy said, 'It's just a little surprise we're planning.'

I think it's about the disco and that Shazia's in on it too. Sometimes the three of them are in a huddle.

Phoebe looks really miserable though.

Another thing. Neither of them has asked me what I'm wearing, which is odd because they usually inspect what I'm going to wear several days before. I think they worry I'd go in my tracksuit if they didn't. And after school when Shazia came round mine – to practise at goal I thought – she wanted to practise *dancing*.

Well, I did my best to show her some steps but I wasn't really in the mood. It might have helped if she'd told me what was going on, but when I asked her she just giggled.

I've a good mind not to go to the stupid disco.

Saturday

Daisy

It went wrong, horribly horribly wrong!

I should have listened to Phoebe. There wasn't a single hour yesterday when she didn't say, 'Are you sure about this, Daisy?' And I snapped back at her every time, '*Yes!*'

But I wasn't really. I had my doubts all along. Even though Shazia's excitement was catching, and I was so excited about wearing her *shalwar kameez*.

I did ask Shazia several times if *she* was sure, and she said, 'Yes, I am certain. Please, Daisy, this is my big chance to be like everyone else, and you know you want to wear my *shalwar kameez*.'

Luckily she didn't mind that I'd told Phoebe, not when I explained why.

It started off OK. Phoebe and I arrived at

school just before six o'clock. I was wearing my sparkly blue skirt and my silver top. Phoebe was in her shimmery rainbow-coloured skirt and top. We'd walked to school on our own, but Phoebe's dad was going to pick us up at eight o'clock when the disco ended. Loud music was already coming from the school hall and it wasn't long before the doors opened.

We waited in the entrance till Shazia and Erika arrived. We knew Erika's mum was dropping them off. Then Shazia and I shot into the toilets and changed. I *adored* wearing her beautiful *shalwar kameez*. It made me feel so special and I couldn't stop looking at myself in the mirror.

But Shazia gasped when she saw herself in my clothes again. The skirt looked even shorter on her because she has long legs. Then she giggled and said, 'Come on, Daisy.'

She almost dragged me into the hall. The

curtains were closed so it was dark except for the disco lights flashing.

'What the . . .?' said Erika when she saw us. For a few minutes she was speechless. Then she said, 'You do realise this could ruin everything, Daisy? *Everything.*'

I said, 'Shut up.' But I don't think anyone

else heard.

Several girls near enough to see said we looked great.

Phoebe looked worried. She hardly danced all evening. I don't think her eyes left the clock in the hall. But even that didn't stop things going wrong.

Phoebe

All I can say is that I did my best, but DISASTER STRUCK!

Mr Majeed arrived at seven o'clock, *a whole hour* early!

I saw him first because I was standing near the door to the entrance hall, looking up at the clock which was just above it. He came in and scanned the room looking for Shazia. I saw him think he'd spotted her at the back of the hall and take a step towards the middle of the room – *towards Daisy*. With the disco lights flashing, all he could see from the door was the sparkles of the *shalwar kameez*, not who was wearing it.

Oh no. I held my breath.

I thought he was going to walk over right then, but he must have thought better of trying to make his way through all the bopping bodies because he stopped and looked around for a teacher.

My breath came out in a spurt as I realised I had to warn Shazia. Warn them both. Where was Shazia? If I could get to them before Mr Majeed, they might have time to get to the toilets and change their clothes.

Now Mr Majeed was talking to Mrs Davies, who was looking straight at Daisy. Oh no. She started striding towards her, and dancers parted to let Mrs Davies through. Could I get to Daisy first?

No one stood aside to let *me* through. The hall had never seemed so long, or the bodies so close together, as I weaved in and out of the dancers, with the music drumming in my ears. But at last I reached Daisy.

Just before Mrs Davies.

I hoped Shazia had escaped to the toilets.

Daisy

Suddenly I felt my arm being tugged.

Phoebe was hissing in my ear. 'Daisy, go to the toilets . . .'

Mrs Davies stood just behind her and was bellowing, 'Shazia, I'm sorry but . . .' Luckily she couldn't see my face because Phoebe was in the way.

'Toilets!' Phoebe hissed again. 'Swap back with Shazia!'

'Your father is here . . .' shouted Mrs Davies.

I saw him, Mr Majeed, at the side of the hall, and realised the danger.

I ran across the hall, out into the lobby, then into the toilets, where I hoped Shazia was waiting.

'Shazia!' I yelled at the cubicle doors.

No reply.

'Have you seen Shazia?' I asked a couple

266

of girls who were gathered round one of the mirrors.

They shook their heads.

I turned as the main door opened.

'Shazia?'

But it was Phoebe looking as if she was being pursued by a raging monster.

'Is . . . Sha—?' She could hardly get the words out.

'No,' I shook my head and dived into a cubicle as the door opened again and there stood Mrs Davies.

'Girls, what's the matter?'

Phoebe – I don't know how she thought of it – said, 'Shazia's upset, Mrs Davies. She put a bit of make-up on and she thinks her father will be angry.'

There was a silence. Then Mrs Davies said, 'Well, tell her to wipe it off quickly and come out. Her father is waiting.'

I heard the door close and thought, *What do we do now?*

Erika

As soon as I saw Shazia in Daisy's disco skirt and top I knew something would go disastrously wrong and it did.

I'll never forgive them for not telling me what they were up to. Never. And Dais is the one who prides herself on being so sensible!

I can't forget the moment Shazia realised her dad was in the room. One minute we were dancing in a group with a few others. Next she stopped suddenly, her arms in midair.

I said, 'What's up?'

But she didn't reply. She just turned round and shot off, dodging between all the moving bodies. Did she need the loo in a hurry? I looked round – and saw Mr Majeed standing by the door.

And there was Phoebe staring up at him, looking white and shaky.

Catching on, I looked in the opposite direction. Well, Shazia wouldn't have rushed into her furious father's arms, would she? I couldn't see her in the dark, but I headed for a door on the other side of the hall. Was she in the corridor?

No.

What now?

I opened one of the classroom doors leading off the corridor and called out, 'Shazia, come out! It's me, Erika. Let's find Daisy and swap back before your dad sees you.'

No reply.

Well, I must have looked in every classroom – the corridor went right round the hall – till I found myself back in the lobby. I was behind Mr Majeed and Mrs Davies who were talking to each other.

The front door was open. Could Shazia have run out past them?

But where to?

As I stood behind the grown-ups I heard Mr Majeed say, 'I am bringing such a very nice surprise for Shazia. Her grandmother has arrived from Pakistan for a holiday. That is one of the reasons I wanted her to wear her very best *shalwar kameez*.'

Then the door to the toilets opened and two girls came out. Through the open door I saw Phoebe beckoning frantically and I dashed inside.

Phoebe whispered, 'Go and get Shazia. Daisy's ready to swap back.'

I whispered, 'Can't. I've looked all over the school. She's disappeared.'

Phoebe

I felt terrible. I mean, I was supposed to be looking after Shazia.

I said, 'She must be somewhere.'

But where? I started to rack my brains.

Erika said, 'Where's Daisy?'

'Here,' mumbled Daisy from behind the cubicle door, 'And here's the *shalwar kameez*.' A bundle appeared under the door. 'Listen. We've got to find Shazia. It's best if we all look. Can you find me something to wear?'

All I could see was a bin bag, lining the bin. Luckily there were only a few tissues in it.

'Sorry, Daisy, it's all I can find,' I said as I shoved it under the door. I pushed the *shalwar kameez* back too. 'You'd better hide this under it.'

Honestly, when she came out . . . Any other time Erika and I would have laughed ourselves silly, but there was too much to do. I'd had a hunch where Shazia might be. I could hear her voice saying, *'This would be very good for a game of hide-and-seek.'* Where were we when she'd said that?

Suddenly I remembered – on the playing field after Toddlers' Group, when my mum told us about how the Monsters got stuck *under the stage* where they keep the ride-on toys in the village hall.

Would she hide there?

It was the only place I could think of so we made a plan.

Daisy

When Mrs Davies saw me step into the lobby her mouth fell open.

Erika said, 'Dais has spilled Coke all over her new clothes, Mrs Davies. She thinks she should go home and put them in the washing machine straight away.'

Mrs Davies frowned. 'And Shazia?' She looked at Phoebe. 'Is she er . . . ready?'

'Nearly,' said Phoebe breezily. 'She'll be out in a minute.'

Mr Majeed was laughing as we edged towards the door. 'I do hope Shazia does not want to be wearing the latest bin-bag fashion. Her Daadi-ami would not approve.'

Mrs Davies was still frowning. 'Girls . . .'

I think she was going to say we shouldn't be going home alone. Or question us about Shazia. But it was too late. We were outside.

I just hoped she wouldn't go into the toilets and look for Shazia – or come after us.

Phoebe strode ahead. When we got out of sight of the school we ran.

Luckily the village hall wasn't far – it took us about three minutes to reach it – and the door was open. We could hear grunts and gasps from the badminton players as we stood in the entrance. When Phoebe opened the door to the main hall we saw shuttlecocks flying around.

Nobody stopped us as we crept round the sides of the hall to the stage. We had excuses ready – we were looking for the bag Phoebe's mum had left at Toddlers' Group – but no one asked.

So everything went smoothly.

Except that Shazia wasn't under the stage.

Erika

So much for Phoebe's amazing hunch!

As we removed the panel at the front to reveal tractors and tricycles and a ride-on turtle, I prayed Shazia would crawl out.

She didn't.

Daisy called Shazia's name, but there was no answer.

She whispered, 'Come out, Shazia, if you're in there. We've got your *shalwar kameez*. If we move fast we might be able to get you back to school and er . . .'

She didn't say what the rest of her plan was.

Daisy crawled under the stage – and out again. We all helped put the panel back.

As we walked out of the hall the badminton match ended.

A lady called out, 'Find what you wanted, girls?'

Phoebe shook her head. I think she was close to tears. I was desperate for the loo.

Apologising for delaying the others, I dived into the ladies'.

And there was Shazia, crouched in a corner!

Phoebe

I was nearly right!

It didn't take long to get Shazia out of Daisy's disco clothes and into her *shalwar kameez*. Daisy put her own clothes back on and went to shove the bin-bag in the waste bin but I stopped her.

'We need that.'

We raced back to the school gate and hid behind the wall, where we could see Mrs Davies and Mr Majeed in the entrance.

Now for the hard bit – getting Shazia inside without arousing suspicion.

'Hitch up your *shalwar*, Shazia.' I meant her trousers. Then I put the bin-bag over her head, covering her completely.

Daisy and I took hold of her arms and we led her to the door.

Erika stayed behind the wall.

279

Of course Mrs Davies looked up as we got near the door. So did Mr Majeed.

'What on earth . . .?'

They both looked confused, but laughed, which is what we wanted. We were ready to say it was Erika trying out the new bin-bag fashion but we didn't need to. We dived into the toilets and whipped the bin-bag off Shazia, who rushed out again and into her father's arms.

'Abu-ji! Did I hear you say Daadi-ami is here? Let's go home *now*!'

Mrs Davies went into her room and we hurried into the hall. After a few minutes Erika joined us and we had a massive group hug.

Phew!

Friday

A Week Later

Shazia

The minutes that I passed in the village hall seemed like hours. Soon I wished that I had not panicked and run away from the disco. But I knew Abu-ji would be angry to see me in the disco clothes, because I had disobeyed and deceived him. That is why I ran – right out of the school and into the village hall. But then I did not know what to do, till my new friends found me.

Wonderful friends! Daisy and Phoebe and Erika helped me so much.

I have not seen them quite as often this week, not after school, because I am spending time with my darling Daadi-ami. But next week it is clubs and teams once again and on Saturday afternoon I am doing Hula Hoop Club with my three best friends.

Daadi-ami is happy that I have such wonderful friends.

We are like the Famous Five. There's Daisy, Phoebe, Erika, me and Rolly the wumply dumply dog!

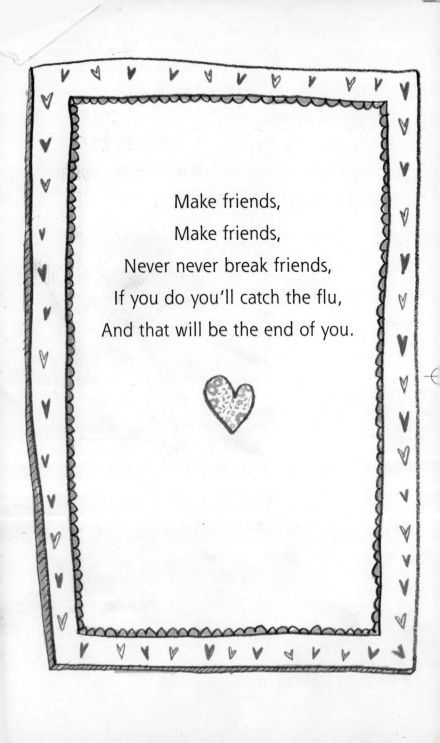

Make friends,
Make friends,
Never never break friends,
If you do you'll catch the flu,
And that will be the end of you.